HER
OWN
SONG

Books by Ellen Howard

Circle of Giving
When Daylight Comes
Gillyflower
Edith Herself
Her Own Song

HER OWN SONG

ELLEN HOWARD

A Jean Karl Book

Atheneum   New York

Atheneum
Macmillan Publishing Company
866 Third Avenue, New York, NY 10022
Collier Macmillan Canada, Inc.
Printed in the United States of America
10   9   8   7   6   5   4   3   2

Designed by Barbara A. Fitzsimmons

Library of Congress Cataloging-in-Publication Data
Howard, Ellen.
Her own song/Ellen Howard.
—1st ed. p.   cm.
"A Jean Karl book."
Summary: When her adoptive father is hospitalized after an
accident, Mellie is befriended by Geem-Wah, owner of a Chinese
laundry, who holds the key to the events surrounding Mellie's birth
eleven years ago.
ISBN 0-689-31444-2
[1. Adoption—Fiction. 2. Chinese Americans—Fiction.]
I. Title.
PZ7.H83274He 1988
[Fic]—dc19   88–3393   CIP   AC

For Mama,
whose song I sing

The author wishes to thank Idalene Simmons and her family for sharing her story.

The author is also grateful to the Boys and Girls Aid Society of Portland, Oregon, the Chinese Consolidated Benevolent Association of Portland, Oregon, and George W. Leong, and especially Ruthanne Lum McCunn, for their help.

Special thanks are also due to the following people for their loving encouragement and criticism: Charles Howard, Margaret Bechard, Susan Fletcher, David Gifaldi, Patricia Hughey, Eric Kimmel, Tobi Piatek, and Terri Zagone.

Contents

HER
OWN
SONG

June 1908
Dreams and Memories

"The laundry cart's coming! The laundry cart's coming!"

Mellie looked over her book and saw two boys speed past hollering, headed for the street. Children were converging in that direction from all over the playground.

Lois McMahon ran past, her cheeks pink with excitement. "C'mon, Clara. C'mon, Jean," Lois was calling to her two best friends. Lois paused for a moment as Clara and Jean ran up to link arms with her. She glanced at Mellie. "C'mon, Mellie," Lois called. "Let's have some fun with the Chinaman!"

Wondering, Mellie got to her feet, leaving her book open on the grass. Lois McMahon had noticed *her*. Lois McMahon had called to her! The smile Lois had thrown over her shoulder as she and the other girls raced away had seemed genuinely friendly.

Suddenly Mellie's heart was skipping, and she felt her own cheeks go pink.

"Hey, wait," she called after them as she took to her heels, holding her hat with one hand. "Wait for me!"

The Chinese laundry delivery cart was creaking past

the school behind its plodding, spavined horse when Mellie reached the sidewalk. The boys were running alongside and behind it, jeering. The girls jumped up and down on the sidewalk, their voices shrill.

"Chinky, Chinky Chinaman!" they shouted. "Yellow-face! Pig-tail! Rat-eater!"

Mellie saw Lois McMahon glance at her. Lois's mouth was open, shouting. Mellie could see her small white teeth and the flash of her pink tongue. "Chinky, Chinky Chinaman!" Lois was shouting.

Mellie took a deep breath, and something stirred in her middle. "Yellow-face," Mellie shouted with Lois. "Pig-tail! Rat-eater!"

A stone hurtled from somewhere and struck the horse on its shoulder. The blow interrupted the horse's discouraged gait. It turned its head, and Mellie thought it looked at her reproachfully. Then its head went down, and the horse began to plod again, a little faster.

"Getty-up," the Chinese man was yelling. "Getty-up!" He shook his fist at the boys. "Velly bad boys," he cried. "Bad, bad boys!"

Lois was laughing at the man's antics.

Mellie laughed, too. She pointed at him. "Look, Lois, look what he's doing now," she cried, and was rewarded when Lois looked and then laughed harder.

It was then that Mellie saw the Chinese girl.

She was huddled beside the man on the seat of the cart, and she cringed against him as though terrified. As

Mellie caught sight of her, the girl turned her head and cast a frightened look at the schoolchildren. Mellie had an impression of a thin, pale face—pale tan, Mellie thought, not yellow at all—and two dark, frightened eyes.

Something about those eyes caught Mellie like a blow in the stomach. She had seen them before!

"Chinky, Chinky Chinaman!" the children were shouting, but suddenly Mellie was not shouting with them. She was staring at the long, black pigtail that swung against the girl's thin, blue-jacketed back as the laundry cart turned the corner, away from the school. She was remembering. . . . Remembering?

. . . reaching for a shining, silken plait of hair that swung above her like a charm as someone bent over her singing, as someone lifted her into warmth, into light. Nuzzling her face against that fragrant, ginger-scented hair. . . .

She was remembering?

"Yellow-face!" the children were shouting. "Pig-tail!"

Mellie turned away from the shouting voices, her stomach sick. It wasn't like that! Not nasty, the way the voices made it sound: "Pig-tail! Rat-eater!" In her head, she could hear the voices taunting her.

"Adopted!" the children used to tease, when they were younger. "Mellie's a poor little orphan. Got no mama. Got no papa. Had to be adopted!"

"I do too got a papa," Mellie used to cry, stamping her foot.

But the children had an answer for that. "Not a real papa," they said. "Not a really *real* papa."

The taunts had turned to whispers as they grew older, but Mellie found the whispers no easier to bear.

"Is it true, Papa?" she had asked her father when the teasing first began.

Papa had turned his head, not meeting Mellie's eyes. "I care for you like you *was* my own," he said.

Now, tears in her eyes, Mellie found herself running away from the shouting children. She ran toward the tree where she had left her book. She could feel her tears against her cheeks, cold in the breeze her running made. Her hat flew off.

She slammed against the trunk of the tree, clinging for a moment to the rough bark, and then she looked back.

The children had formed into a circle for a circle game, and in its center, directing the game, was Lois McMahon, imperious as a queen.

All afternoon in school, Mellie felt so embarrassed she could scarcely lift her gaze from her desk. What in the world had possessed her to run away like that when the children were teasing the Chinaman at noon recess? It was the first time ever that Lois McMahon had invited her to join them, and she had behaved like a ninny! Now Lois would probably never speak to her again. Mellie had missed her chance to be included at last.

Mellie stared miserably at the page of her arithmetic book, but the numbers jumbled together and she could not sort them out. She kept thinking about noon recess and the way she had behaved. No wonder the other children didn't like her! She *was* different—odd, as the other children whispered. None of *them* were bothered by a laundry cart horse's reproachful look! None of *them* felt sorry for a Chinky China-girl! She *was* weak-stomached and soft-hearted, as Papa often told her. "You got to toughen up, Mellie-girl," he said. "Life ain't like it says in books. You got to be hard."

The dismissal bell jangled into Mellie's thoughts. She jumped and then glanced about to see if anyone had noticed. But no one paid her the slightest attention. They were slamming desk tops and gathering books and bolting for the door. Clara and Jean and two or three other girls crowded around Lois McMahon and begged to walk her home.

"I believe I'll walk with Clara today," Lois proclaimed. "Clara and I have things to discuss."

The other girls turned away, disappointed. Clara's freckled face glowed as she and Lois walked to the door together.

Mellie was fiddling with her book bag, pretending to be intent on fastening its leather straps. She wanted to wait until most of the children were gone before she attempted the walk across the school yard. Although so far today they had ignored her, she knew from experience it took only one boy or girl to start the snickering, the too-loud whispers that proclaimed her difference. "Adopted. She's adopted, you know. Poor Mellie Langford!"

Yet when Mellie trailed across the empty playground a while later, she found herself almost wishing there was someone there to tease her. She felt so lonely.

Was it simply the fact that she was adopted that made her different from the others? Or was it something else? Something to do with the dreams she had sometimes, and the almost-memories? Like the way the Chinese girl's eyes made her feel this afternoon. Like the picture that came to her head when she saw the long pigtail. . . .

Mellie shook her head as though to shake the vision away. She had never seen that girl before. She knew she never had! The Chinaman was always alone in his cart, Mellie was sure, and Mellie had never seen any other Chinese in East Portland. Even the Chinaman didn't *live* here. He came from the laundry in Chinatown, across the Willamette River, to deliver and pick up the washings of the neighborhood families. He picked up Papa's overalls and heavy work shirts and their sheets and towels and tablecloths.

Aunt Estie said it wasn't worth doing the plain laundry at home, the Chinaman was so cheap, and though Papa grumbled that cheap to Estie meant it was *his* money being spent, Aunt Estie had her way, as she usually did in household matters.

Papa said Frances had always done all the laundry herself, and Aunt Estie said, well, *that* was Frances, but she wasn't a slave to any man, least of all to her own baby brother. Bending over a washboard was likely what killed Frances anyway, she said.

Papa's face got dark then, and he said Aunt Estie didn't know anything about it and to shut her face.

And Aunt Estie said, well, and *that* was all the thanks she got for stepping in to help raise this poor orphan he and Frances had taken in in a fit of foolishness!

And Papa said Aunt Estie ought to be glad of a home when no other man would have her.

And then Aunt Estie got red and said, *well!* and stomped off to her room and wouldn't come out for the rest of the day.

Now, at the corner of the schoolyard, Mellie pushed away thoughts of Papa and Aunt Estie and Frances, the adoptive mother she scarcely remembered. She slung her books over her shoulder and looked both ways to make sure no wagons were coming. The street was empty, except for some boys dawdling on the next corner, a block away. Mellie sighed. It was a long walk home, and she was late getting started. She would have to hurry if she was going to have time for her chores before supper.

I

THE
LOCKET

Frances,
Six Years Before

Her hand plucked at the bed sheet restlessly, but her eyes never left the door. In a moment, Bill would come, bringing her little girl. Only a moment, she told herself. Only a moment more and I can see her, can look at her just once more.

"Just once more, Bill," she had begged him. "I want to give her my locket, to remember me by. I had her such a little time, she's likely to forget."

"Later, Frannie," he had protested. "You're all wore out. Y'ought to be savin' your strength."

She had looked at him, a long, silent look. "For what, Bill? Save my strength for what?" and then she had been sorry for saying it, when she saw the defeated slump of his shoulders and the way he turned wordlessly away and went to fetch the child.

The door was opening. Frances saw Bill's hard-corded arm pushing it open and holding it so that Mellie—My precious Mellie, just turned five, Frances thought—could walk through.

Frances held out her hand, trembling, to the child, and slowly Mellie came to the bed. Bill stood in the doorway, and

Frances did not look at his face, for fear of what she would see.

"Precious," Frances said, and she could hear how breathless was her voice, how weary and weak.

"Hullo, Ma-ma," the child said, her blue eyes wide and serious. She spoke in her odd, singing accent that had so charmed Frances the first time she heard it. "I hope you feel better today."

Frances forced her lips to a smile. She touched the child's face, touched the soft fair skin with her fingertips. She closed her eyes for a moment to gather strength and then opened them and said, "Yes, dear heart, I do . . . I do feel . . . much better."

The child gazed at her solemnly.

"Is . . . Aunt Estie . . . taking good care of you?" Frances managed to whisper.

"Yes . . ." The child paused, as though to consider, and put her own small hand to Frances's cheek. "Yes, but I like better when you take care of me, Ma-ma," she said, and her words caught at Frances's heart. Such a little time, there had been such a cruelly little time to take care of her, after waiting so long.

Frances struggled to nod and closed her hand over Mellie's. There was no strength left for talking. But she held fast to the child's hand. There was something she was forgetting, something she must give her. Something Mellie must always remember.

The child was looking at Bill. "Papa?" she was saying.

And Bill was moving to the bed, in one long anxious stride.

Frances could not bear the grief and pain and fear in his face. She let her eyes close again.

"Come, Mellie-girl, Mama is tired," Bill was saying.

But Frances kept tight hold on the little girl's hand. She moved her head on the pillow and fought to draw breath.

"Love . . ." Her lips were forming the silent words. "Know . . . I . . . love . . ."

Frances could not hear her own voice. She reached for the thing she was forgetting, but it was gone. She could feel Bill's hands on her shoulders, lifting her up, shaking her. She could hear his voice calling, but she could not answer. She was too tired. Too tired. And too far away.

She heard Mellie crying. . . .

Aunt Estie's Holiday

The Chinese girl would not leave Mellie's thoughts. She kept seeing those dark, scared eyes in her mind all the way home from school that day, and as she did her chores.

"Here, chicky chick," she called to Papa's chickens as she scattered their grain, and she heard in her mind the children's taunts: "Chinky Chink! Chinky Chinaman!"

"Squeek-squawk, squeek-squawk," went the pump when she drew water for Aunt Estie, and in her mind she heard the creak of the laundryman's cart.

And as she spread the blue cotton tablecloth and laid the table for supper, she kept remembering the long, black pigtail that swung against the Chinese girl's blue-cotton-jacketed back.

"You're mighty quiet this evening, Mellie dear," Aunt Estie said at supper.

Papa grunted and reached for the bowl of turnips. "That's as should be," he said. "Leave the girl alone."

Papa was eating intently as he always did. Although

he was small and thin and taut as a fiddle string, he loaded his plate two or three times at every meal and ate every bite, polishing his plate at the end of the meal with a piece of bread, which he also ate, and then asked for pie.

Aunt Estie, on the other hand, was big and soft and ample, yet she ate sparingly in small, thoughtless bites tucked between the words that gushed from her mouth like water from a pump.

Aunt Estie was always trying to "draw Mellie out," but Papa said "children should be seen and not heard." Mellie didn't know how to please them both.

"Well, she looks a mite off to me," Aunt Estie said crossly. "Are you feeling ill, Mellie dear?"

"I'm fine," Mellie said, trying to sound fine.

Oddly enough, Aunt Estie did not pursue it. An unaccustomed quiet settled over the table. The noise Mellie made drinking her milk sounded loud in her ears. Papa chewed steadily, his eyes on his plate. Nervously, Mellie stuffed her mouth with the beans and new potatoes Aunt Estie had dished out for her. She chewed and chewed, but she couldn't seem to swallow.

Aunt Estie gazed into space, a little frown between her eyes. Her fork hovered uncertainly. Finally, she put it down.

Mellie laid down her fork and looked at Aunt Estie. Only Papa continued to eat, unperturbed.

Aunt Estie cleared her throat, and Mellie jumped.

"Brother," Aunt Estie said, and Mellie knew it was something serious. Aunt Estie only called Papa "Brother" when matters of consequence were discussed.

Was it about her? Mellie wondered. Had she forgotten to latch the chicken yard gate? Had she neglected the kindling box, or smoked a lantern, or torn a hole in a frock? *Had someone tattled about teasing the Chinaman?* Mellie pressed her hands together to keep them from trembling.

"Brother," said Aunt Estie, "I am going to take a trip!"

Papa reached for the bread basket and selected a thick, brown slice.

"A trip," Aunt Estie said, her voice louder. She lifted her chin and challenged the top of Papa's bent head with it. "A holiday," Aunt Estie said. "I've never taken a holiday."

Papa lifted his eyes and mildly surveyed Aunt Estie's flushed face. Then he reached for the butter crock and scooped out a big dollop with his knife.

"Mellie is quite old enough to see to the house while I am gone," Aunt Estie said. "School will be out before I leave, and I'll show her what to do. You'll get along fine. Just fine."

"By yourself?" Papa said around a mouthful of buttered bread.

"With Emma and Louise Jenkins," Aunt Estie said. "To Far Rockaway Beach. For the month of June."

"Them!" Papa said, dismissing Aunt Estie's lady-friends with a snort. "Any pie tonight, Ess?"

Aunt Estie snatched up her fork and speared a green bean. She popped it into her mouth and chewed furiously. She drained her tumbler of tea. She took her napkin from her lap and folded it, slowly, into her napkin ring. Then she pushed back her chair. "Clear the plates, Mellie dear," she said.

Mellie slid off her chair and began to gather the plates, still trying to take it all in. Aunt Estie was going away for a whole month without them. She, Mellie, must see to the house. They would get along fine, Aunt Estie said. And Papa wanted his pie! Mellie made a neat stack of the plates and followed Aunt Estie toward the kitchen.

"Rhubarb," Aunt Estie said shortly to Papa as she pushed through the swinging door.

"And some coffee, Ess, if you please," Papa said, pushing back his chair.

It was all muddled in Mellie's mind as she lay in the dark that night, waiting for sleep. The Chinese girl's frightened, familiar eyes that somehow made Mellie feel frightened, too. Aunt Estie at the beach in a woolen bathing dress. The spavined horse. The laundry cart. The irate laundryman. And Papa, eating rhubarb pie as though Aunt Estie had announced a shopping trip. As though nothing were out of the ordinary. As though nothing at all had happened that day.

But nothing *has* happened, really, Mellie thought. I *am* almost eleven, plenty old enough to see to the house. And it will be *nice* for Aunt Estie to have a holiday. And it was *only* a crazy Chinaman . . . and a stupid China-girl. . . .

The tears slid cold down Mellie's cheeks and puddled cold in the curves of her ears. She reached . . .

Somewhere quite near was a soft, ringing sound and the silken swish of something bright, something that caught the light and held it in a shimmer of warmth. She tasted sweetness in her mouth, smooth on her tongue, and felt the breathing nearness of someone who was singing. The singing, the strange, familiar singing lulled her toward sleep, so near she had only to reach to make the song her own. She reached . . .

She reached for the sound, for the light, for the taste and touch, for the voice she could almost hear. Was it Frances? she wondered. Frances singing that odd lullaby? Or was it someone else? Someone before Frances . . . Mellie hugged herself close.

The room was high-ceilinged and cold and dark. There was no one there.

Aunt Estie was to leave on Saturday, the day after school let out for the summer.

When Mellie came home on Friday, full of the news

that she had been promoted to sixth grade, Aunt Estie was not in the kitchen fixing supper. Mellie found her upstairs in her bedroom. Aunt Estie's empty portmanteau, open on the bed, peeked from among heaps of ruffled petticoats. Shawls and chemises and shirtwaists in neatly folded stacks overflowed dresser, chair, and commode. Aunt Estie herself was half-buried in hatboxes hanging from one arm and dresses draped on the other. Her new straw hat was on her head.

"Should I wear this hat, do you think, Mellie dear?" she said. "It's apt to be sooty on the train."

Mellie opened her mouth to say she thought the new hat was perfectly lovely, but Aunt Estie's voice rattled on without pause. "No, I'd best wear my old gray with the gray tulle veil. It won't show the soil." Aunt Estie dumped the hatboxes on top of the petticoats and began lifting lids, searching for the gray hat. The dresses slid with a whisper to the floor. She seemed to have forgotten the hat on her head.

"I got promoted," Mellie said.

"Here it is!" cried Aunt Estie. "Now what did I do with my gray parasol?" She waved the hat and turned her head from side to side as though expecting the parasol to appear magically in the air. "Oh dear," she said, suddenly spying the dresses at her feet. "Oh dear, oh dear, I'll have to press these again if I don't mind what I'm doing." She clapped the gray hat atop the straw one already on her head and swooped to pick them up.

"Can I help?" Mellie said.

Aunt Estie was spreading the dresses on top of the petticoats and hatboxes, a pile as precarious as the hats on her head. "Parasol. Parasol," she was muttering.

"I think it's in the umbrella stand," said Mellie.

Aunt Estie glanced in Mellie's direction. "Run fetch it for me, will you, dear?" she said.

Mellie slipped through the doorway and ran for the stairs. Behind her she heard Aunt Estie's voice.

"Promoted?" Aunt Estie said. "That's nice."

Mellie started down the stairs.

"And my black umbrella, Mellie dear," she heard Aunt Estie call.

The house felt strange to Mellie when she and Papa returned from seeing Aunt Estie and her lady-friends and their hatboxes and portmanteaus and trunks and bags and baskets of food off on the train.

For as long as Mellie could remember, Aunt Estie had always been in the house, talking, clattering, singing, complaining. Aunt Estie was the *sound* of the house, Mellie thought, and then told herself, She's only gone for the month of June.

But Papa wanted his dinner, and so Mellie was busy right away and stayed busy with washing up and loading the woodlift and tidying the house and planning what to set out for supper. And then there was supper to get from the food Aunt Estie had cooked up ahead and washing up again and getting out the lamps for Papa to light.

It was a warm evening, but not so warm that Papa wanted to sit on the porch, so they sat by the library table lamp in the sitting room. Mellie had a library book, and Papa had his paper. Soon Mellie was yawning and, though Papa didn't send her to bed as Aunt Estie would have done, pretty soon Mellie was going up the stairs, the little lantern in her hand, feeling odd because Aunt Estie wasn't rustling up behind her, complaining that Papa never *would* have gaslight laid on, he was so close.

So Saturday passed and Sunday passed with Mellie feeling busy and very grown up. She gave scarcely a thought to the summer about to begin, and she tried not to hear the silence of the house, and she certainly didn't allow herself to think of the dark, frightened eyes of the Chinese girl.

Monday, the Accident

It was a dream Mellie had had many times—actually one of two dreams. But Mellie didn't like to think about the other one.

This dream was nice. When Mellie awoke Monday morning, it lingered behind her closed eyelids, and she tried to hold it fast. But even as she realized she was awake, the dream was slipping away. The sound of it was growing faint, just a soft tinkling—a sound like crystal striking crystal when she dried and put away the glassware in the dining room buffet. And yet, that wasn't quite right either, Mellie thought, squeezing her eyelids shut and willing the dream to stay. It was a warmer, mellower sound than crystal, and it was closer to her ear and filled with warmth and scent. . . .

Mellie thought she was naming it as she opened her eyes, but the sound and the dream were gone. In their place were the slamming of a screen door and footsteps on the porch beneath her window and the warmth her own body made in the coolness of the sheets, and the smell of coffee in the wood-smoky morning air.

Mellie sat upright in bed.

Papa, she thought in alarm, suddenly aware of the brightness of the sunlight through her window. It was late. She had overslept. This was Monday and, though she didn't have to go to school, Papa would be going to work. She should be up to fix his coffee.

She jumped out of bed and ran to the window, her heart sinking even before she caught sight of Papa on his bicycle headed down the wooden sidewalk. She was too late.

Why hadn't she gotten up? Why hadn't he called her? Already she was failing in her duties as lady of the house.

Mellie watched Papa turn the corner, his thin shoulders hunched over the handlebars. His lunchbox was in the basket, she saw, and the coffee smell in the air told her Papa had made his own coffee to carry to work.

Monday was laundry day.

When Mellie hurried down to the kitchen for a slice of toast and a mug of milk and coffee, her head was full of the things she must do before Mrs. Prucha arrived to help with the washing. The water must be heated in the boiler in the basement. The beds must be stripped, the towels and tablecloths changed. The basket at the foot of the laundry chute must be emptied and the clothes sorted. Those to be sent to the Chinese laundry must be bundled for the laundryman's cart.

For the rest of the day, Mellie planned to be useful and busy, just as Papa would want her to be. When Papa came home, the laundry would be done and supper would be special and ready for the table.

Mellie couldn't wait to finish breakfast. She bustled down into the basement, still chewing a mouthful of toast, to light the burner and put the water on. She decided to ready the laundryman's bundle first and set it on the kitchen porch for him. She would be occupied in the basement with Mrs. Prucha, she thought, and likely wouldn't see him. Yes, that was the thing to do, she thought. Get the Chinaman's bundle ready first. She needn't see him or his cart or his horse. . . . She needn't see again that China-girl. . . .

Still, she did see the Chinese man.

Mrs. Prucha had finished the washing by noon. She and Mellie had lunch at the kitchen table. After the steamy basement, the kitchen seemed wonderfully cool.

"So," Mrs. Prucha kept saying, her bosom heaving with melancholy. "So your auntie has gone to the seashore, is it not? So. For a holiday." Mrs. Prucha wiped her mouth and then her whole face with her napkin. "Fine ladies have holidays so," she said. "So. It is the way with ladies such as your auntie. So."

Mellie was glad when Mrs. Prucha had finished eating and sighing. "I can finish hanging out the clothes,"

Mellie told her, handing her the money Aunt Estie had left.

"Remember, Miss Mellie, to bring them in before dark," Mrs. Prucha warned. "So. And watch for rain." She squinted at the cloudless sky. She mopped her shining face again, this time with her handkerchief.

"I will," Mellie promised.

"A holiday may be spoiled by rain," said Mrs. Prucha hopefully. "I have heard it rains often at the seashore so. Yet your auntie *will* have her holiday, is it not so? So," she said sighing. "So."

Mellie waved Mrs. Prucha down the alley.

"Next Monday," Mrs. Prucha called. "So?"

The laundryman's bundle was still on the kitchen porch. Mellie looked up and down the alley. There was no sign of his cart.

It took only a moment to wash up the lunch dishes. Hanging out the clothes took a little while more.

Mellie knew what she wanted for Papa's supper. She would go to the meat shop to get him some calf's liver. Papa loved calf's liver fried up with bacon and onions sliced thin.

Mellie took off Aunt Estie's apron. She tidied her hair, smoothing it back from her face and retying her hair ribbon. She put on her sailor hat and counted out some coins from the black leather purse of housekeeping money.

Feeling very grown-up, she stepped out on the front porch and closed the door behind her, then looked up and down the street for the laundryman's cart. It was nowhere in sight.

Mellie hurried down the steps and set off for the meat shop, keeping a sharp eye out for coins that might have fallen between the cracks of the wooden sidewalk. The Chinaman would surely come while she was away, she thought.

Still, she found herself peering anxiously toward her house as she came back around the corner a little while later, the package of calf's liver dangling from her hand in Aunt Estie's string bag. Her heart skipped a beat when she saw the laundry cart waiting at the entrance to the alley. This is silly, she told herself. There was no one waiting on the seat of the cart and . . . He wouldn't remember *me*, she thought, out of all the children who teased him that day.

She made herself continue walking toward her house, watching for the laundryman to come out of the alley. Yet she couldn't help slowing, just a little. Possibly the Chinaman wouldn't even see her as he carried the bundle to his cart, she thought. He *could* drive away before she reached home.

And then she caught sight of the boy on the front porch. It was a boy she had never seen before, a boy with a shock of sandy hair and a blue work shirt and worn blue overalls.

He was talking to the laundryman, who stood beside him, the laundry bundle slung on his back.

The boy saw her at the same moment she saw him. "Do you know where I might find the folks what live in this here house?" he called.

The laundryman stepped back, into the shadows of the porch.

"I live in this house," said Mellie.

"Oh," said the boy, looking flustered. "This here *is* Bill Langford's house, ain't it?"

"Yes," said Mellie, beginning to climb the steps. "He's my father."

"Oh," said the boy again. "Ain't your ma to home?"

"No," said Mellie. It was simpler than explaining. "No," she said. "I'm the only one here right now."

The boy looked troubled. He dug his hands into his overall pockets and frowned.

Mellie saw that the laundryman was edging toward the steps. Good, she thought. He shouldn't be on our *front* porch.

"Well," said the boy. "Reckon I'd best tell *you* then, Miss. Now don't take this hard. . . ."

Mellie stepped up onto the porch, moving aside for the laundryman. She was looking at the boy.

"See, I'm from your pa's work," the boy was saying. "There's been a accident."

The laundryman stopped on the second step. He

was looking at his feet, but Mellie had the feeling he was listening.

"An accident?" she said.

"Your pa," said the boy. "He got hurt, and they said I should run and tell his folks quick."

"Hurt?" said Mellie. Why didn't the Chinaman go? she thought.

"They've took him to the hospital," the boy said. "They sent me to tell his folks."

Mellie groped for the banister. "Papa?" she said, holding onto the banister hard. "Papa hurt?"

"Your pa *is* Bill Langford?" the boy repeated.

Mellie nodded her head.

"Yep," said the boy. "They said to tell you they was takin' him to the hospital, and you should come right away."

"Right away," Mellie repeated, but all she could think of was how important it was not to let go of the banister.

"That's right," the boy said, edging toward the steps. "I'm right sorry, Miss, but they said to tell his folks."

"Thank you," Mellie said. She was waiting for her heart to start beating again. "Thank you for telling me."

The boy brushed past the laundryman and ran down the steps, then headed down the sidewalk at a fast clip. He was almost out of sight when Mellie felt her heart stir. The hospital, it thumped faintly. The hospital, the hospital, the hospital.

Mellie started suddenly. "Wait," she called, running down the steps after the boy.

But the boy was far down the street. He did not stop.

Mellie stared helplessly after him, the string bag of liver dangling uselessly from her hand. "Which hospital?" she was crying. "Which hospital did they take him to?"

Geem-Wah

A streetcar clanged past down on Union Avenue. Mellie could not see it, for it was several blocks away, but its noise roused her.

The boy was gone. She stood, halfway down the steps, staring at the place where she had last seen him. A delivery wagon turned the corner behind a sturdy mare. A neighbor came out on her porch and cupped her hand to her mouth as she called to her child. A boy chased a cat up a tree.

Mellie turned and, automatically, began to mount the steps again. She would go in, she thought. She would put the liver in the meat safe and take off her hat. . . .

But her way was blocked by the Chinese laundryman.

His eyes were not cast down. They were turned straight on her—sharp, black, with a look of . . . pity, Mellie thought. How dare he pity *me*!

"Why are you looking at me like that?" she demanded. "Why don't you be on your way?"

"Missy go hospital?" the man said.

"It's none of your affair," Mellie said.

The laundryman bowed his head, but he did not move out of Mellie's way.

"I don't know which one!" Mellie cried, suddenly close to tears. "That stupid boy didn't tell me. Oh, what will I do now? How can I find out?"

The laundryman didn't answer.

Mellie's mind was beginning to race from thought to thought, snatching them up and throwing them down again. How could she find out where Papa was? There were several hospitals in Portland. She was not even certain where they were. If only she had asked! Perhaps if she went to the factory, they could tell her . . . but Mellie had never been to Papa's workplace. She knew it was down by the river. She knew he bicycled there. Aunt Estie would know. She ought to get in touch with Aunt Estie . . . except she didn't know exactly where Aunt Estie was either. Aunt Estie was to send a postcard as soon as she was settled in a hotel or boardinghouse, but it might be days before a postcard arrived from Far Rockaway Beach. Perhaps Mellie ought to call up somebody. Mr. Tilzer, the across-the-street neighbor, had told Papa they might use his telephone if ever they had the need. But Papa didn't hold with telephones, any more than he held with imposing on neighbors, and Mellie didn't know how to talk on one. And whom could she call?

Suddenly Mellie was wishing that Frances had not died. Frances would not have left Mellie alone at a time

like this. Frances would not have gone off on a holiday
without her. . . . But Frances *had* died, just as, Mellie
supposed, her real mother must have died. They had taken
Frances to the hospital, Aunt Estie had told Mellie, and
she had come home again only to die.

The hospital.

Mellie felt a hand on her arm.

"Missy," the Chinese man was saying.

Mellie burst into tears.

With one part of herself, Mellie knew it was the
Chinese laundryman who was lowering her to the step,
his arm strong and gentle about her shoulders. With one
part of herself, Mellie knew that he shouldn't have dared.
. . . But another part of herself was comforted. Another
part of herself put her head against his chest and sobbed
and sobbed and sobbed.

"Better soon, Mei-Li," the Chinese man murmured.
"Don't cry. Don't cry, Mei-Li, don't cry."

Mellie cried against the laundryman's chest until
she was empty. His voice murmured in her ears with a
gentle, sing-song lilt that was strangely comforting. It
was some minutes before it occurred to her that he was
speaking English as plainly as she did. His silly-sounding
pidgin had disappeared.

She pulled away, wiping her cheek with the flat of
her hand and frowning. "What happened to your accent?"
Mellie said. "That's not the way you usually talk."

The Chinese man was regarding her steadily. Mellie

could not read his expression. Did that slight twitch at the corner of his lips signal a smile?

"No," he said softly. "I do not usually speak this way to foreigners."

"You mean that Chink-talk is just put on?" Mellie demanded, outraged.

The Chinese man bowed his head, and Mellie was sure now he was hiding a smile.

"It is expected," he said.

Suddenly, Mellie remembered where she was and what had just happened. She sprang to her feet and backed away from the Chinese man, across the porch toward the front door. "Why are you hanging about like this?" she said. "What if someone sees you?"

As she said it, Mellie realized how awful that would be, to be seen talking to a Chinaman, *crying in a Chinaman's arms* on the front steps. She caught her breath. Aunt Estie would have a hissy fit!

Her eyes searched the street and sidewalk and the yards of the neighbors' houses. The lady and her child had gone indoors. The boy and his cat were nowhere in sight. The street was empty. In the still, hot middle of the day, she imagined the little children must be taking naps and the ladies planning their suppers and the men not yet home from work. She let out her breath.

"You'd best go on," she said, blushing to think that only a moment ago she had been touching him. What had possessed her? Whatever had she been thinking of?

Of Papa, her heart answered her with a turn. Of Papa lying in a hospital somewhere. Hurt. Maybe badly. Maybe . . . Her mind turned away from the thought.

"What will you do?" the Chinese man was asking. "How will you find your father?"

"I . . . I don't know," Mellie said.

"Where is your aunt?"

Mellie glanced nervously down the street again. "You'd better go," she said, a little desperately. "Someone might see you." Might see *me* talking to you, she was thinking, and she saw something flash in his eyes. Anger? Or was it fear?

"You are correct, of course," he said. "I should not be seen talking at length with a child of foreigners, a *lo fahn*." He stepped farther back into the shadow of the porch, kicking aside the bundle he had dropped behind him. "Still, I cannot leave a child in trouble," he said. "Where is your aunt?"

Mellie waved her hand, wondering vaguely how he knew that Aunt Estie was not her mother. "Gone," she said. "Gone away."

"When will she return?"

Mellie knew she should not be telling a stranger, especially the Chinese laundryman, her private family business. Still . . . She searched his eyes, which were looking deeply into hers. Still . . .

"Not for a long time," Mellie said. "Not for a month."

"A month," the Chinese man said. "Can she be telegraphed?"

"I don't know where she is," Mellie said, tears starting to her eyes again, and then she was telling him the whole thing—how she had to wait for the promised postcard to know Aunt Estie's hotel, how she couldn't think who might be able to help her find Papa, how she didn't know what to do.

"Are there no other relatives?" the Chinese man was asking. "No neighbors? No friends?"

But Mellie shook her head, feeling more and more helpless by the minute. There was only Papa and Aunt Estie. Papa never brought anyone home, and Aunt Estie's lady-friends were at the beach with her. Mellie's mind shied from asking the neighbors for help. Papa didn't hold with being too friendly with neighbors. "They mind their own business and I mind mine," he said when he was provoked with Aunt Estie for "taking up" with them. No, there was no one, no one Mellie could think of, to help.

The Chinese man stood, his head bowed and his arms folded, and said nothing. Once or twice he shook his head. Then he raised his eyes and looked at Mellie again. "Come, Mei-Li," he said. "It is evident that I, Geem-Wah, must help you to find your father."

The springless cart lurched and bumped over the ruts in the street. Mellie thought her teeth would be jarred from her head, and her bottom was sore from bouncing on the hard wooden floor of the cart. She huddled among the bundles of dirty laundry, trying to keep her head low as the laundryman, Geem-Wah, had instructed her, but the noisy creak and rattle of the cart seemed destined to call attention to the fact that she, Mellie Langford, was riding in a Chinese laundry cart.

"What if someone sees me?" she had asked him when he told her of his plan.

"I do not think they will," he said. "Most *lo fahn* do not truly see the washee-washee man."

Mellie had to admit the truth of this. How many times had she seen the laundry cart on its rounds in the neighborhood, and yet never really *looked* at it?

"We will go to all the hospitals," Geem-Wah had said, "until we find your father."

It had seemed so simple when he explained it to her. He would wait outside, pretending to be picking up laundry, while she went in to ask. When they found him, Papa would tell her what to do next.

So now Mellie rattled along in the cart, keeping her eyes on Geem-Wah's narrow, black-jacketed back and his jouncing, long pigtail, and tried to keep from biting her tongue between her jarring teeth. She tried not to think about how badly Papa might be hurt.

Geem-Wah hauled on the reins, and the horse ambled to a halt.

"We are here, Mei-Li," Geem-Wah said, not looking back. "I will tell you when the coast is clear. Stay low."

He climbed out of the cart and went to the horse's head. Facing her, he seemed to be doing something to the harness. Mellie saw him smile at her, a reassuring smile. His eyes ranged quickly around.

"Now," he said quietly. "You may get out now, Mei-Li."

The Hospital

"Are you sure this is the hospital?" Mellie asked Geem-Wah.

"When Yeen-Fu's son was struck by the Meier and Frank wagon, they brought him here," Geem-Wah said.

Mellie looked at the run-down building in its overgrown, weedy yard. The windows of the building looked blank.

"What happened?" she said.

Geem-Wah looked at the ground. "He died," he said.

Mellie stared at the building.

"Go quickly, Mei-Li," Geem-Wah whispered urgently, busying himself once again with the horse's harness.

Mellie saw an old man limp around the corner of the building, staring at them curiously.

Mellie's feet moved, heavy with dread, one in front of the other. They carried her away from the cart and toward the door of the hospital. Her hands twisted together.

The old man disappeared. Mellie had to open the door by herself.

The woman Mellie found at a desk inside the door was brusque and hurried. "We've had no accident cases today," she said. "Is your father destitute?"

"Destitute?" Mellie said.

"Destitute," the woman snapped. "Without money. Poor. This *is* the county hospital, you know."

Mellie, appalled, shook her head. She hadn't known.

"No doubt he was taken to a private hospital," the woman said crossly. "Try Good Samaritan or that place run by the nuns." She turned away and was absorbed again in the papers on her desk before Mellie could think what to say.

Mellie swallowed her questions and tiptoed to the door, embarrassed. She was almost relieved she hadn't found Papa here.

Good Samaritan Hospital was built of neat red brick. It looked clean and cared for. But at Good Samaritan, the only person Mellie could find to ask was a black man, sweeping the lobby. It was the first time she had ever spoken to a black man, and she had trouble understanding his thick, slow voice. But his shaking head told her what she needed to know. Papa was not at Good Samaritan either.

The black man did not turn away from Mellie as the county hospital woman had. His big, yellow-rimmed eyes followed her to the door. Mellie could feel their sympathy, like a warm touch, even when she was outside again, hurrying toward Geem-Wah's cart.

At the hospital run by the nuns, St. Vincent's, the great double doors seemed too high, too wide, much too heavy for someone Mellie's size to open. She stood before them, at the top of the stone entrance stairs, and could not bring herself to take another step.

What if he isn't here either, she thought. This was the last big hospital in Portland, Geem-Wah had said. After this, they would have to begin on the clinics and the sanitariums, whatever they were.

"Surely he will be at St. Vincent's, Mei-Li," Geem-Wah had reassured her, talking over his shoulder as they jounced along the rutted street away from Good Samaritan. "It is not far from here. I have heard that the sisters are kind."

Perhaps the sisters were kind, but standing on the stoop before the tall entrance doors, Mellie almost turned away. It was too much—more than she could bring herself to do—to push open those doors and go inside this building, as imposing as the county hospital had been dilapidated. Going inside would mean questioning yet another kind of stranger. First a Chinaman, then a Negro, and now nuns. I have talked to too many strange kinds of people, Mellie thought, remembering how Aunt Estie was always cautioning against strangers. He won't be here anyway, she decided. She turned her head and looked down the street where the laundry cart awaited her,

Geem-Wah pretending to be busy with the bundles in the back. It looked almost welcoming, the laundry cart. Almost *comfortable* . . .

Just then the great doors swung open, and Mellie was knocked backward by two billowing black figures who swept out onto the steps.

"I beg your pardon," a voice was saying. Gentle hands were steadying her, and Mellie was looking into the plain, friendly face of a girl not very much older than Mrs. Prucha's girl, Eva, who was just sixteen. Only *this* girl was dressed all in black and white, and a large wooden crucifix swung from a chain round her neck.

"Are you all right?" the girl, who was a nun, was saying. "Did we hurt you, bowling you over like that?"

"I . . . I'm fine," Mellie said. "I shouldn't have been in the way."

The other nun retrieved Mellie's hat, which had been knocked from her head. She held it out. Mellie took the hat and jammed it on her head, trying not to stare. She had never been so close to a nun. They smelled of yellow soap and starch.

"May we help you, dear?" the girl nun said, and there was something in the tone of her voice and in the way she called Mellie "dear" that made Mellie's throat feel tight.

"I . . . I'm . . . looking for my father," Mellie said, and then, in a rush, "Is he here? Did they bring him here?"

"Come inside," the older nun said.

The inside of St. Vincent's Hospital was wide and high and flooded with light. Mellie felt very small. She wished her shoes were clean.

"Come this way," the older nun said, leading Mellie to a high, marble counter behind which a nun in spectacles worked. There were several wooden chairs beside the counter. The nuns made Mellie sit down in one of the chairs. The older nun sat down, too.

"Now—calmly—tell us your name and your father's name and why you think he might be here," the older nun said.

Mellie held her hands tightly clasped in her lap and made her voice as clear and calm as she could and told them.

The girl nun was looking questioningly at the bespectacled nun behind the counter. The bespectacled nun nodded. "The concussion on Ward Three," she said.

"Yes, of course," the older nun said. "Your father is here. He was brought in, injured, around noon. I settled him into bed myself, not an hour ago."

Mellie burst into tears.

Through her confusion of worry and relief and embarrassment, Mellie was surprised to see the girl nun hold out a handkerchief to her. She wouldn't have thought a *nun* ever needed to blow her nose.

Mellie took the handkerchief and scrubbed at her

eyes. Self-consciously, she blew her nose. Papa was here! She had found him! This was no time to be crying.

"Is he badly hurt?" Mellie said. "Is he going to die?"

"Oh, heavens, no!" the girl nun said.

The older nun glared. "What Sister Rosalie means to say is that God's will shall be done," she said sternly. "We will hope for the best . . . and pray."

Mellie looked at the older nun, then at Sister Rosalie, whose eyes were fixed on the floor. "How badly is he hurt?" Mellie repeated, balling the handkerchief in her hand.

"A blow to the head," the older nun said briskly. "An industrial accident, I believe."

"He is unconscious," Sister Rosalie said quietly, "but I heard Dr. Kavanaugh say his chances of recovery are good."

The older nun glared again, and Sister Rosalie fell silent.

Mellie looked at the balled-up handkerchief in her hand. It was grimy with dirt from her hands and wet with her tears and snot. She closed it in her fist, hiding it, and felt vaguely ashamed.

"May I see him?" Mellie said.

Sister Rosalie leaned forward, opened Mellie's hand, and took back the handkerchief. "I'm sorry," Sister Rosalie said.

"That is quite impossible," the older nun was saying. "Quite out of the question. Children are not allowed."

"Mellie," Sister Rosalie said, "he would not know you were there. He is unconscious."

"But I have to take care of him," Mellie said.

"*We* will take care of him," the older nun said.

"But I *have* to see him! I have to!" Mellie's throat was aching so hard she could scarcely whisper the words.

"Your mother can see him," the older nun said. "Where *is* your mother?"

It came to Mellie suddenly just what they were saying. Papa was unconscious.

Unconscious.

That meant Papa couldn't tell her what to do, even if she did see him. It meant he couldn't come home with her. It meant Mellie was all alone.

"Where *is* your mother?" Sister Rosalie was echoing, and without thinking, Mellie answered what she always answered when people asked her about her "mother."

"She passed away when I was five."

Alone.

"Oh, I *am* sorry," Sister Rosalie was saying, and the older nun was shaking her head thoughtfully.

"I suppose, while your father is in the hospital, our sisters at the orphanage might find room for you," the older nun said.

Mellie drew in her breath sharply, suddenly alert. Orphanage? She didn't want to go to an *orphanage*! She wanted to go home!

"Oh, no," Mellie said quickly. "I can't do that. My aunt lives with Papa and me."

Both nuns looked at Mellie, their eyebrows arched. In the corridor nearby, something rattled past on squeaking wheels. Mellie heard voices, funereal and low.

"She . . . my aunt, I mean . . . Aunt Estie . . ." Mellie's thoughts were racing faster than her tongue could follow. "Aunt Estie wasn't home when the message came this afternoon, so I came looking for Papa myself," she said. It was the truth, she thought. Aunt Estie *wasn't* home.

The nuns were looking at her. "Alone?" the older one said.

Mellie saw her mistake. "A . . . a friend brought me," she said. That also was the truth, she thought, surprised. "He . . . he's waiting for me outside."

"Won't your aunt be worried not to find you at home when she returns?" Sister Rosalie said.

Mellie started up. "Oh, yes," she said. "Yes, I really must go home."

The nuns walked Mellie back across the foyer, telling her what to tell Aunt Estie about when she might come to visit. Mellie looked, but could not see what had made such a rattling and squeaking in the corridor. They passed

two men in black frock coats. A white-aproned nurse
scuttled by.

"We'll just see you safely off," said Sister Rosalie
as they neared the door. "You're certain that your friend
is waiting?"

Mellie thought of the laundry cart parked down the
street. "He's waiting," Mellie said, "but . . ." She
searched her mind frantically for a reason the nuns should
not see her to the cart.

Sister Rosalie pushed open the door, and the older
nun ushered Mellie outside.

Mellie glanced desperately down the street. The
laundry cart was there, parked in front of a top buggy,
and Geem-Wah sat on the seat.

"Where is your friend?" the older nun said.

"There," Mellie said, flinging out her arm. "There
he is!" She pointed toward the buggy.

"Where . . ." Sister Rosalie said, and just then a
man in a white duster walked around to the front of the
buggy and climbed in.

"There. There," Mellie cried. She bobbed a curtsy
as Aunt Estie had taught her and ran down the steps.
"Thank you," she called over her shoulder.

Mellie raced down the sidewalk toward the buggy.
Once she glanced back. The nuns, at the top of the steps,
gazed after her.

Geem-Wah was looking at her as she ran past the

cart. She darted into the street between the cart and the buggy horse, as though she were going to the street side of the buggy. Instead, glancing once more at the nuns, Mellie flung herself into the back of the cart. "Hurry," she cried. "Hurry, Geem-Wah. Let's go!"

Chinatown

He was crushing her. His stink was choking her. His darkness covered her eyes. He was taking her away, and she did not want to go. He was taking her away from the light and the song. She could not breathe. She could not see. She could not move, and she struggled to be free. She struggled and she screamed and no one came. . . .

Mellie opened her eyes, her heart thumping hugely in her chest. Geem-Wah's kind face was leaning close to hers. His hand was on her shoulder, shaking her.

"Wake up, Mei-Li," he was saying. "We are here."

Mellie sat up, shaking her head to clear away the bad dream. "We are here," Geem-Wah was saying, but where was "here"?

Mellie peeked over the side of the cart. It was dusk, and the street lamps cast pools of warm gaslight at every corner of the street that stretched before her. It was a street from another world!

Geem-Wah was helping her out of the cart, a hand under her arm. "Come, Mei-Li," he was saying. "We shall go to my house to eat, and then I will take you home."

"I . . . I must have fallen asleep," Mellie said. "I must have fallen asleep in the cart."

"You have had a tiring day," Geem-Wah said. "So much worry and sadness, so much traveling here and there. . . ."

And so many new people and places, Mellie thought, looking about her at this new place. The street was filled with people, and yet there was not one person who looked familiar to Mellie. Many of them were dressed much as Geem-Wah was dressed, in loose trousers and high-buttoned jackets and low, cloth-soled shoes. A man walking past on the sidewalk wore a bowler hat like Papa's, but a long, black pigtail like Geem-Wah's dangled beneath it. A woman dressed in trousers like a man followed behind him, holding the hand of a little boy whose clothes were the colors of the rainbow and whose eyes were shiny black in his round, brown face. Chinamen, Mellie thought. All Chinamen.

As Mellie followed Geem-Wah across the wooden sidewalk, her head kept turning from side to side. The brick buildings were fronted with rickety balconies festooned with all manner of odd things. The shop they were passing displayed strings of vegetables and baskets of eggs and a row of plucked birds, glistening with oil. Mellie made her way around huge baskets heaped with fruit, and tripped over a wooden crate that was decorated with beautiful, curling symbols painted in red.

Geem-Wah steered Mellie into an alley between two buildings. Mellie would not have known it was there if Geem-Wah hadn't pushed at a high wooden wall, which, Mellie saw when it swung open, was a gate. A torch in a bracket flared at the end of the alley.

Mellie shivered, although the evening was warm. She slipped her hand into Geem-Wah's. She knew she shouldn't have done such a thing, but she couldn't help herself. The dank air of the alley seemed to close in around her with its smell of privies and foreign cooking, and something sharp and sweet that seemed strangely familiar. Her knees wobbled as she walked down the alley, but Geem-Wah's hand was warm and strong.

Near the end of the alley a door stood open in the brick wall. From it came the damp smell of soap and bleach and the dry, hot smell of scorching cloth. Geem-Wah led Mellie through the doorway into a low-ceilinged room, lit by smoking lamps. The room was filled with Chinese men, standing at ironing tables and crowded by baskets of laundry. The men were all chattering at a great rate, it seemed to Mellie, but one by one, they fell silent as Geem-Wah and Mellie threaded their way between the tables and the baskets of laundry.

Someone called out in a voice that seemed to Mellie ugly and threatening. The other men muttered, but Geem-Wah said something, and they ceased to mutter and watched Mellie with eyes that made her want to turn and run.

Geem-Wah said to her, "Don't be afraid. They will not hurt you." He held her hand firmly.

Then they were through the ironing room and in a narrow hallway that led to a steep wooden staircase.

"This way," Geem-Wah said.

Mellie's heart beat fast. She did not like the darkness or the smells or the musty air of the stairwell. Why had Geem-Wah brought her to this place? For the first time, it occurred to Mellie that Geem-Wah knew she was alone, knew Papa was too hurt to protect her, knew no one would know for a very long time if she did not come home. Mellie's feet stumbled on the slippery stairs, and she felt Geem-Wah's hand tighten on hers. She remembered again that Geem-Wah was a Chinaman, like all the other people in this place, and she was only a girl, a young, white girl. Mellie had heard that Chinamen preyed on white girls, that they did terrible nameless things to them. "White slavery," Mellie had heard, and "opium dens" and "darkest Chinatown."

Chinatown.

She, Mellie Langford, was being led up these stairs into the darkest of dark corners of darkest *Chinatown.*

She could feel the panic swelling in her chest, squeezing her heart, cutting off her breath as in her dream. She was twisting her hand free of Geem-Wah's strong hand. She was opening her mouth to scream . . .

when Geem-Wah pushed open a door at the top of the stairs, and Mellie looked into the eyes of the Chinese girl.

The girl started back from the door, and Mellie saw in her eyes a reflection of Mellie's own fear. For a moment, Mellie thought it was Geem-Wah who frightened the girl—He is going to hurt me *and* the China-girl, she thought—and then she realized it was her, Mellie, the girl was staring at.

Geem-Wah was talking, and another person, an old woman, was coming out of the shadows of the lamplit room. The old woman caught sight of Mellie and began to screech, her voice rising wildly, like the agitated sound of an over-wound gramophone.

Mellie realized her own mouth was open. She closed it and swallowed hard.

The old woman had come close. She was no taller than Mellie. Her face was as smooth and golden as a piece of yellow soap, but her tiny hands flailed as she spoke, and her voice was shrill.

Geem-Wah spoke to her, his words quick and loud and, Mellie thought, angry. His hand slashed the air.

The old woman fell silent. She looked at Mellie, her eyes hard and slitted.

"This is my old mother," Geem-Wah said. "You may call her Liu Tai."

Liu Tai glared.

Mellie found herself dropping a curtsy, as though

she had been introduced to one of Aunt Estie's lady-friends. "How do you do?" she said, feeling huge and clumsy and out of place.

"This is Oi-Lin," Geem-Wah said.

The Chinese girl ducked her head, still looking frightened. "How do you do, Mei-Li," she said haltingly in English.

Mellie was watching Liu Tai. Going to the small stove in the center of the room, Liu Tai was banging pot-lids and muttering beneath her breath as she scooped rice into a bowl. The smell of the steaming rice caught Mellie like a blow in the stomach. She had not realized how hungry she was.

Liu Tai ladled broth and vegetables from another pot.

Mellie sat down on the bench by the stove that Geem-Wah indicated. Her legs collapsed beneath her at the last minute, so that she sat heavily. As she put out her hands to take the bowl Liu Tai shoved at her, she remembered the liver she had bought for Papa's supper—days ago, it seemed. Had it been only this afternoon that the messenger boy had been waiting on the steps? She and Papa would have been finished with supper by this time of night, she thought, if Papa hadn't been hurt. If *only* Papa hadn't been hurt!

Mellie held the bowl, warm in her hands, and the hunger turned to sickness in her stomach. Who would get Papa's supper now? Who would see that he ate it? If

only Aunt Estie were here to go visit him, to make certain
he was taken care of. If only the nuns would let her,
Mellie, see him, just for a minute. If only he would wake
up!

Oi-Lin was offering Mei-Li two slender sticks.

"You eat with them, Mei-Li," Geem-Wah said.
"Like this." Mellie saw him lift his own bowl to his
mouth and use the sticks to push the food into it.

Mellie put down her head and concentrated on trying
to hold the sticks as Geem-Wah was doing. Her fingers
cramped. Her hand, which was holding the bowl, was
trembling. She was going to spill her food!

She became aware of Oi-Lin's slim hand helping to
steady the bowl under her chin. Oi-Lin was placing the
fingers of her other hand around the sticks more com-
fortably. Somehow, the food was beginning to find its
way into Mellie's mouth. It was rice, flavored with the
broth and vegetables, hot and good. The smell and the
taste filled Mellie's nose and mouth, and she began to
chew and swallow greedily. Her stomach began to feel
quiet and warm. Her hands stopped shaking. She looked
gratefully at Oi-Lin, but the girl would not meet her
eyes. When she saw Mellie could manage by herself, Oi-
Lin went to sit next to the old woman on the other side
of the stove.

Geem-Wah passed Mellie's bowl to Liu Tai to fill
twice more. Each time, the old woman grumbled and

clattered the pot-lids. Yet when Mellie had finished, she gave her a small bowl of pale tea.

Mellie sipped the tea, which smelled and tasted different from Aunt Estie's orange pekoe, and looked about her at the small, cramped room that was Geem-Wah's home. The beds were two narrow cots against one wall. The shadowed shelves of the cupboard were stuffed with baskets and boxes and bundles and bowls. Mellie noticed a tablet on one shelf, with some odd little sticks smoking before it. The tablet was inscribed with graceful curling symbols like the ones on the crate on the sidewalk. The smoke from the stick smelled sweet and bitter at once, like the smell she had noticed in the alley. A low counter leaned against the third wall. Under it were baskets with lids and a wooden barrel with a cover.

Suddenly, Mellie knew that the barrel held rice. You scoop it with a shiny, rainbow-colored shell, she thought. Her eyes opened wide, and she caught her breath and stared at the barrel. Geem-Wah and his old mother were quarreling again, and Oi-Lin was drinking her tea with small slurping sounds. These sounds, the smells, and the very room itself were familiar to Mellie. She knew them, had always known them, but did not know how she knew.

II

THE

BRACELETS

Lan-Heung,
Seven Years Before

Her hand automatically dipped the rice from the rice barrel with her abalone shell measure. She poured the rice slowly into her pot, listening intently to the sounds downstairs. Something was wrong, she thought, but she was not certain what had told her so. She could hear the voices of the men who were playing pai-gow in the back room. They seemed undisturbed. It was the street sounds that were different, hushed. Lan-Heung's jade bracelets rang softly in the unusual quiet as her hand dipped and poured the rice, and every part of her stood alert.

"Thus?" Mei-Li was asking. "Do I fold the paper thus to make a crane, Ma-Ma?"

"Hush, little one," Lan-Heung said. "Hush for a moment. Ma-Ma is listening."

Mei-Li, at play on the floor, cocked her head and listened, too. Her blue eyes were big. Her funny little plait of brown hair poked untidily from beneath her cap. Lan-Heung smiled fondly at the little girl.

Then, suddenly, she heard the shouts. It was Brother-in-law who was shouting, and then the unintelligible harshness of a lo fahn's *voice. There was a crash and the sound of feet pounding up the stairs.*

Lan-Heung dropped her abalone shell and was at the door in an instant, thrusting home the bolt. She stumbled to Mei-Li and snatched her from the floor and retreated, staggering, to the far side of the room. She paid no attention to the pain in her tiny, bound feet, or to her cane, which she had left beside the rice barrel.

Someone was banging on the door. Someone was shouting in the harsh, unmusical language of the lo fahn. *Shouting and banging on the door.*

Lan-Heung cowered in the farthest corner of the room, clutching Mei-Li to her.

"What is wrong, Ma-Ma?" Mei-Li was crying. "Who is knocking at our door? Who is calling so loudly?"

Lan-Heung held the child more tightly, rocking her. "Hush, hush," she murmured, her eyes fixed in terror on the door, which vibrated from the blows on the other side.

"Ma-Ma, I'm scared," Mei-Li cried, hiding her face against Lan-Heung's breast. "Make him go away, Ma-ma!"

The door splintered and gave inward. A huge, black-booted foot kicked through the shattered wood. An arm, a shoulder, a long leg clad in dark blue came through the broken door.

Lan-Heung stared in horror, unable to look away from the giant lo fahn *who had forced his way into her house.*

He was calling to someone else, someone in the stairwell,

and then there were two lo fahn *in the room, leering at her.*

Lan-Heung sank to the floor, her bound feet no longer able to bear both her weight and the child's. Mei-Li's arms clutched around her neck. Lan-Heung heard a whimpering sound and did not know if it was the child or herself who made it. Where was Husband? she thought in anguish. Why did he not come to save them? Was he dead? Had the lo fahn *killed him, and would they now kill her and her child?*

Lan-Heung pulled off her bracelets and slipped them over Mei-Li's plump hand, pushing them up her little arm inside her sleeve. My Lady, she prayed to the goddess of mercy, protect my child's life. Protect her from devils with these circles of jade.

The lo fahn's *hands were upon her. His hands were big and pale and hairy. Repulsive, barbarian hands! He was trying to wrest the child from her.*

"Don't hurt her," Lan-Heung was crying. "Do what you will with me, but, I beg you, don't hurt my child!"

The lo fahn *pulled Mei-Li from her arms.*

Mei-Li was screaming. "Ma-Ma," she cried. "Ma-ma!"

The lo fahn's *mouth opened, flashing a golden tooth. The sounds of his barbaric language were as coarse as his thick, white skin. He turned, handing Mei-Li to the other one. They were taking her away!*

It was then that Lan-Heung understood why they had come. They had come for her child. They had come for Mei-Li! Lan-Heung fell forward onto her knees. She raised her hands in supplication.

"You cannot take her," Lan-Heung cried. *"She is mine, my own thousand pieces of gold. My husband bought her four years past. We have a paper to prove it so."*

The lo fahn *were stepping back through the shattered doorway. Lan-Heung saw they did not understand.*

"Wait!" Lan-Heung *cried, scrabbling on her knees toward the cupboard where the precious paper was kept. "Wait, and I will show you!"*

But the lo fahn *were gone. Lan-Heung heard their heavy boots upon the stairs.*

"Mei-Li!" Lan-Heung *wept, rocking on her knees.*

She heard the child's voice calling to her from the stairwell. *"Ma-Ma,"* Mei-Li *cried. "Ma-Ma!"*

The cries echoed in Lan-Heung's ears long after silence had fallen.

Tuesday, Dreams

"Take me home!" Mellie cried. "Take me home *now*, Geem-Wah!"

Geem-Wah and Liu Tai and Oi-Lin looked at Mellie, startled. Mellie knew what it was that surprised them. It was the tone of her voice. Mellie could hear it herself. It was the tone of Lois McMahon on the playground when she wanted her way.

"Please," Mellie said more quietly, feeling suddenly ashamed. "Please thank Mrs. Liu Tai for my supper, but I am very tired. I really must go home."

Geem-Wah put down his tea bowl. His eyes searched Mellie's in a way that made her look down, embarrassed. She twisted her hands in her lap.

"Of course, Mei-Li," Geem-Wah said. "We will go now."

Mellie did not fall asleep again in the laundry cart. She huddled in its bottom among the bundles of dirty clothes Geem-Wah still had not unloaded and watched the cold stars in the sky overhead. It was not chilly, but she clenched her teeth together to keep them from chat-

tering with the rattling of the cart, and she hugged
herself.

In the silence of the night, the cart's racket was
unbearably loud. Downtown, the horse's hooves rang on
the paving, and when they drove across the Burnside
Bridge, Mellie could hear their hollow sound echo from
the water below.

Once, someone hailed the cart. "What you doin'
out so late, John?"

Mellie flattened herself in the bottom of the cart,
eyes closed to make herself invisible.

"Fo-gettee to fetch laundlee fo velly big lady,"
Geem-Wah said in his put-on pidgin. "Gottee go gettee.
She have John's hide!"

Mellie heard an unpleasant laugh and the smack of
a hand against the horse's rump. The cart lurched forward.

"Well, you better hurry, John, you know what's
good for you. Funny things can happen to a Chinaman
out so late."

"Yes-yes!" Geem-Wah cried, his voice loud and
high. "John go velly fast. Yes-yes!"

Mellie let go her breath, shakily. What would happen to Geem-Wah if he was caught with a white girl in
his cart? Would they send him to jail? Suddenly she
thought she understood why old Liu Tai had seemed so
upset when Geem-Wah brought Mellie home with him.
Geem-Wah had been taking a risk to bring her there. In
fact, he had been risking bad trouble all day, helping

Mellie. If they were discovered, Mellie wondered, would anyone listen when she tried to explain?

For that matter, what would happen to *her* if it was discovered that she had been left alone? They might send me to an orphanage after all, Mellie thought. The idea horrified her. Her arms prickled with goose bumps, and the blood pumped so loudly in her ears that even the rattling of the cart was muffled. Hurry, she started saying under her breath. Hurry, Geem-Wah. Take me home.

Yet at home, when they had drawn up in the alley beside the house where Mellie thought it less likely they would be seen, she was suddenly even more frightened. It was all she could do to make herself climb out of the cart to go into the dark, looming house.

Geem-Wah did not get down from his seat. "Go quickly, Mei-Li," he said over his shoulder. "I must hurry back."

Mellie stumbled to the back gate, felt for the latch, and then turned.

Geem-Wah and the cart and horse were dark shadows in the alley. The horse was snuffling heavily through its nose.

"You are certain you will be safe, Mei-Li?" Geem-Wah whispered through the darkness.

"I'm not afraid," Mellie whispered, knowing that she was.

The reins slapped softly against the horse's back, and the horse wheezed and began to move.

"Good-bye, Geem-Wah, and thank you," Mellie called quietly, watching the retreating shadow of the cart. "Thank you, thank you," she kept saying, even as she turned back to the open gate, even as she stumbled down the path and up the steps to the kitchen porch.

The neglected laundry flapped whitely on the line. The chickens muttered in their coop. Heart racing, Mellie pushed open the kitchen door and felt her way to the matchbox on the wall.

"Thank you, thank you," she was still whispering as she struck a match, her whisper filling the emptiness of the kitchen with sound. She wondered who she was thanking, and for what, as the shadows cast by the flickering match leaped from the walls to meet her. She stood in the middle of the deserted kitchen, holding aloft the match, and realized that for yet another time that day she was crying.

Sometime in the wee hours of the morning, it must have rained. Mellie woke, head throbbing, to an overcast sky and a smell of damp. She had slept heavily, her bed an oasis of safety in the empty, creaking house, but she had the impression of troubling dreams and of being alternately hot and cold. Her throat felt sore, and her eyelids were swollen. She lay, curled tightly on her side, with her face to the window, and watched the gray square of sky and the dripping branches of the weeping birch.

She wondered if she were sick.

If Aunt Estie were home, she would come to see why I don't get up, Mellie thought. She would bring hot lemonade and rub my chest with camphorated oil. She would . . . But thinking of what Aunt Estie would do only made Mellie's head ache. Aunt Estie was at the beach, Mellie thought bitterly. She was having a good time with her lady-friends. No doubt she had not given Mellie a thought since she stepped onto the train. Aunt Estie was not Mellie's mother, after all. No one was Mellie's mother!

I mustn't cry again, Mellie thought. I don't *care* that I don't have a mother. Who needs an old mother anyway? I have Papa and Aunt Estie and . . . But Papa's in the hospital and Aunt Estie's at the beach, said a voice in Mellie's head. They'll be back, Mellie told herself desperately. Perhaps Papa will wake up today. Perhaps the postcard will come. . . .

Mellie flung back the covers and sat up, throwing her legs over the edge of the bed. The shock of cold clamped her shoulders. The floor felt icy to her feet.

Someone should be taking care of me, Mellie thought as she made her way downstairs. She stumbled to the front door to check the mail, but there was no postcard. She sat on the porcelain commode Aunt Estie was so proud of, and the chill of the oak seat seeped into her bones. If I am sick, I should be in bed, Mellie thought, remembering the coziness of her bed upstairs. In bed, the covers once more about her ears, it was easy for Mellie to imagine that somewhere in the house, Aunt Estie might be bustling about the housekeeping. She closed her eyes.

The dreams came and went. She would waken sometimes with screams still echoing in her head and a smothery feeling in her chest and her heart beating hard. Other times, she came to consciousness crying, a crying without tears that hurt in her throat and head. But late in the afternoon, the dreams got better. She woke just before dusk to the familiar good dream, the singing dream, and the colors behind her closed eyelids were the colors of the rainbow suit of the child in Chinatown. Her head was not aching, and her muscles were not tense, and her feet were warm. Tentatively, she swallowed, and her throat was not sore.

Mellie turned on her back and stretched her legs and felt the sheets cool against her warm skin. The coolness felt good. If I had been *really* sick, Mellie thought, if I had been really sick all day, I could have died for all anyone cares.

She turned her head to the window. There was a kind of golden glow behind the branches of the birch. Mellie watched, a heavy, sullen feeling in her chest, as the glow deepened and then faded until the sky was dark. The rain had stopped. Mellie heard a bird singing a twilight song. She heard a wagon roll by in the street, and the voice of a neighbor. The sounds seemed

new to her. All day they had been lost in dreams. In
dreams . . .

Mellie lifted her head off the pillow and sat up on
her elbows to look about her dusk-dim room. The room
swam dizzily for a moment, then righted itself with a
lurch Mellie felt in her empty stomach. Somewhere in
the back of her mind, the dreams were nagging her—
dreams of Papa, still and white in a narrow bed, and of
Aunt Estie in her woolen bathing dress, dancing in the
surf with a black-swathed nun. Mellie had been jolting
along in the cart, searching, searching, searching for the
singing and the lovely, tinkling sound. . . .

But right now, urgently, Mellie was hungry. Very,
very hungry. And so she pushed the dreams away.

This time, when she went downstairs, she built a
fire in the range and found bread and cheese and part of
a pudding Aunt Estie had made. She heated milk for
cocoa.

When at last she was full, her shins toasting before
the open oven door, her cocoa mug cradled in her hands,
she allowed herself to think. She thought of Papa and
wondered how she might find out if he was better. What
must those nuns have thought, when they saw her jump
into the laundry cart? She thought of Aunt Estie at the
beach, Aunt Estie who hadn't remembered to mail a
postcard. I don't care if the old postcard ever comes,
Mellie thought. I will take care of myself until Papa comes

home. In fact, if Papa's still poorly when he comes home, I'll take care of him, too.

But thinking this made a sick place in Mellie's stomach. She swirled the cocoa dregs in the bottom of the mug and sighed. I couldn't even *find* Papa without Geem-Wah's help, she admitted to herself. And that made her think of her journey to Chinatown and the angry old woman, Liu Tai, and Oi-Lin's familiar, frightened eyes. Why do I remember her eyes? Mellie wondered. She thought of the other half-memories she couldn't place— the colors, the song, the tinkling sound. She thought of the way Geem-Wah's language seemed somehow known to her, as though she could understand if only she listened harder. She thought about Geem-Wah's room.

Mellie gathered up her dishes and took them to the sink. How did I know there was rice in the barrel? she thought. How did I know?

Suddenly, halfway to fetching warm water from the range reservoir, she realized that she didn't *know*. I only guessed, she thought. No one opened the barrel and showed me the rice. It might have held flour or sugar or beer. It might have held *anything*.

Then she was laughing at herself. "You are just imagining things," she heard Aunt Estie's voice telling her, as she had told her so many times. "Land o' Goshen, Mellie Langford, where do you get such notions? You are just imagining things, Mellie dear."

Still, Mellie thought, pouring warm water over the

dishes in the sink. Still, I surely would like to know what is in that barrel.

Upstairs again, she adjusted the lamp wick low, but she couldn't bear to put out the light entirely. The lamp was a comfort. She could see its warm pink light through her closed eyelids as she settled herself for sleep, trying not to hear the sounds the empty house made. Mellie breathed in the lamp's smoke-oily smell. The smell followed her into sleep at last, and in her dreams it was a smell both bitter and sweet. . . .

Wednesday, Alone

The next day—Wednesday, Mellie calculated after a little thought—Mellie woke in the silent house to a sense of urgency. The sun was out again after yesterday's swift summer storm. Seeing the sunshine and remembering the rain, Mellie remembered the clothes that had been hung out to dry a long time ago, on Monday, and the chickens, that hadn't been fed, and the kindling box, which was almost empty, and the stove reservoir, which hadn't been filled, and her dishes from the night before, and . . .

Aunt Estie's postcard! Mellie thought with a lurch of her heart. She hurried downstairs in her shift to check once again the little box beneath the mail slot beside the front door. All the letters were for Papa, except one for Aunt Estie; there was no postcard. Mellie looked through them twice, a sort of hollow feeling in the pit of her stomach, before she put them on the hall table and padded out to the kitchen to start a fire.

She would have to draw water from the pump near the back steps before she could start the coffee, and she had to go back upstairs to finish dressing before she could go outside. When finally she opened the kitchen door, she saw that the clothes on the line were wet again from yesterday's rain. What *would* Mrs. Prucha say? Mellie thought, and then she thought rebelliously that Mrs. Prucha needn't know. Still, Mellie must get the laundry in soon. The neighbors would begin to wonder, if they hadn't done so already, and she didn't need neighbors snooping about and butting in. I'm *not* going to any old orphanage, Mellie thought. I can take care of myself. I *will* take care of myself. She wished the sun to shine hotter. Dry fast, she wished. Laundry, dry fast.

The morning and half the afternoon were gone before Mellie had finished all she had to do. She worked steadily, taking care to think only of the work.

Sure enough, Mrs. Henry, the across-the-alley neighbor, had noticed the clothes left so long on the line. "I was beginning to wonder," Mrs. Henry said, leaning on her fence. "Shame on you, Mellie Langford, for being so unreliable. I'm sure Miss Langford thought she could depend on you while she was away." Mrs. Henry clicked her tongue. " 'Course, Mr. Langford should have gotten after you, but then, what can you expect of a man? If housework was a snake, it'd have to bite Mr. Henry before *he'd* take notice. I expect your dad's the same way."

Mellie hung her head, knowing she *should* be ashamed, but somehow only able to feel a peculiar gladness that someone *cared* what she did, one way or another.

"Now then, don't look so hang-dog, Mellie-child,"
Mrs. Henry said. "I won't tell on you. Just try and
smarten up and make your aunt proud. She has little
enough joy, the good Lord knows. That's a good girl."

Little enough joy? Aunt Estie? It gave Mellie pause.
It had never occurred to her to wonder if *Aunt Estie* were
happy or not.

Just before supper time, Mrs. Henry appeared again,
knocking on the kitchen door with a big, warm pie in
her hands.

"I was doing my baking and found I'd made a pie
too many," she said. "I thought you and Mr. Langford
might be missing good pie about now. Miss Langford
does say your dad's right fond of pie."

Mellie took the pie. She could see that Mrs. Henry
was craning to see into the kitchen behind her and she
was proud that it was spotless, the kindling box full, the
fire hot, the kettle on the boil.

"I thank you kindly," Mellie said to Mrs. Henry,
who seemed satisfied with what she saw.

The pie, sitting in the middle of the kitchen table,
made Mellie feel sad. When she had eaten her bite of
supper and done up her dishes, the evening stretched
ahead of her empty and long. She sat in the kitchen—
the sitting room seemed too dark and big—and stared
at the glowing cracks of the range's firebox.

Papa *was* fond of his pie, it was true. Mrs. Henry's
pie might have been the very thing to cheer him if only

Mellie could have taken it to the hospital. If Aunt Estie were home, she would have gone on the streetcar to visit him, Mellie thought. The nuns at St. Vincent's were probably wondering why no one had ever come. They had given Mellie such careful instructions about visiting hours and who might come and how long they might stay. Perhaps by now Papa had awakened and was asking for Mellie. He would be wondering who was taking care of her. He would be telling them that Aunt Estie was at the beach.

And then they would be coming after her, Mellie thought, getting up to add a stick of wood to the fire. They would be coming after her, despite all her efforts, to take her away to an orphanage. Unless Papa was getting well right away. Unless Aunt Estie was coming straight home from the beach. Unless . . .

Mellie flopped back down on the hard kitchen chair and propped her chin on her hand. They hadn't come after her yet, she thought. She had been home all day for almost two days, and no one had come. So Papa must still be unconscious. She tried to picture Papa with his quick blue eyes closed, lying in a bed in the hospital as in her dream. She tried to imagine Papa, who knew everything that went on about him—"That man has eyes in the back of his head," Aunt Estie said—not knowing even that he was in the hospital, or that Mellie was at home alone, or that she had tried to see him, had wandered all over Portland in a Chinese laundry cart trying to find him. Papa not knowing anything of the last three days. Papa unconscious or . . .

The doorbell rang.

Mellie jumped.

It was them!

Mellie's chair fell backward with a clatter. She took a running step toward the kitchen door, thinking only of escape, and then she stopped, her head swinging around. She made herself think.

It *could* be the nuns, coming to take her to the orphanage. That would mean Papa was awake and had told them about her. Or it could mean something else. It could mean that Papa had died, and they were coming to tell her so. Mellie's feet moved unwillingly across the kitchen. She leaned her forehead against the swinging door to the dining room and closed her eyes. She couldn't run away. She had to know.

The doorbell rang again. Mellie opened her eyes, straightened her shoulders, and took a deep breath. She pushed open the door.

It was still light enough to find her way across the dining room and through the archway into the living room without a lamp.

Through the oval glass of the front door, she could see a man standing on the front porch, his cap clasped in his hands. Mellie could not see his face. Still, she let out her breath with relief. It wasn't the nuns.

She opened the door.

The man was dressed in work clothes similar to Papa's. He was as tall and broad as Papa was slight. Mellie thought she might have seen him before.

"Yes?" she said.

"Miss Langford? You'd be Miss Mellie Langford?"

"Yes."

The man seemed embarrassed, or shy. He did not look her in the eye. "We . . ." he said. "The men, that is . . . the men at the factory . . . and Mr. Lucas, of course, was wonderin' if they was anything you and your aunt needed . . . wanted, that is."

Mellie cocked her head, trying to understand what it was that he wanted. The men at the factory? Mr. Lucas? Mr. Lucas was Papa's boss. She had heard him spoken of.

"Papa's factory?" she asked. "Do you mean Papa's factory?"

The man nodded. "Some of us went to see your pa at the hospital. They said no visitors, except for family. Said he was still out cold. That was some knock on the head he took! We all sure was sorry, Miss. It was a accident."

"When?" Mellie said, feeling a rush of excitement. "When did you go to the hospital?"

"This evenin' after work. The others had to get on home, but I said I'd come make sure Bill's family was all right. I'm a single man myself. No hurry to get home. Is they anything I could fetch for you? Do you need groceries or . . ."

Mellie shook her head. "No," she said. "No, I'm—we're just fine. My . . . my aunt is lying down just now." The lie slipped out so easily, Mellie was amazed at herself. She blushed. "Thank you," she said. "Thank you for coming. Did . . . did they say anything . . . at the hospital . . . about how my papa is?

The man shook his head. "No more'n they've told you all, I'm sure. They said he was doin' as well as can be expected, but still out. That's all." The man twisted his cap around and around in his hands. "I'd best get on," he said.

A movement and a sound from the street caught Mellie's attention. A vehicle was creaking toward them. She craned her head and saw the Chinese laundry cart.

"Well," Mellie said, forcing her eyes away from the cart. Her hands fluttered. "Well, thank you again, Mr. . . ."

Mellie wished she could ask the man in to give him a cup of tea. It was what Aunt Estie would have done.

"Harrison, Miss," the man said. "Woody Harrison."

"Thank you, Mr. Harrison," Mellie said.

The cart creaked nearer.

Mr. Harrison turned, then swung back to face Mellie suddenly. "I almost forgot," he said, reaching into his pocket. "We took up a collection," he said, "for the doctor bills." He shoved something into Mellie's hand, turned again, and hurried down the steps.

Astonished by the weight of the purse in her hand, Mellie tried to call after Mr. Harrison. But no sound came from her open lips, and her eyes were drawn once again to the horse and cart, moving slowly past the house, and to the thin, familiar figure on its seat, Geem-Wah.

Papa's Desk Drawer

The laundry cart did not stop. Mellie watched it disappear around the corner in the dusk. Geem-Wah had not turned his head to look at Mellie. Still, as she shut the front door, Mellie felt comforted. Mrs. Henry, Mr. Harrison, even Geem-Wah was keeping an eye on her. They were making sure no harm came to her.

Mellie leaned against the door, suddenly tired. The purse Mr. Harrison had left was heavy in her hand. The fading daylight shadowed the living room. She needed to light the lamps.

Mellie felt her way back to the kitchen. She looked at the shelf where the lamps were kept. They stood in a neat row, shining from the cleaning she had given them earlier that day. Mellie felt proud of the way she was taking care of things. Aunt Estie could have done no better, she thought. She reached for the littlest lamp, the painted tin one with flowers on its base, which Aunt Estie let her use to light the way to bed at night. She took it carefully to the table, its kerosene sloshing softly, and lighted its wick. After replacing the sparkling chimney, and adjusting the flame, she looked once again at the tanned leather purse Mr. Harrison had put in her hand. For the doctor bills, he had said. Of course. The hospital and the doctor and perhaps the nursing nuns would have to be paid for taking care of Papa. We are not *destitute*, Mellie thought.

Mellie opened the purse and shook out a wad of bills and a clatter of coins. It was a lot of money, more than Mellie could remember seeing all together in one place. One by one, she smoothed the crumpled bills. She arranged the coins in piles. Four quarters in a pile, ten dimes, twenty nickles . . . She counted the pennies. Eleven dollars and seventy-one cents! Why, that was enough to buy the solid gold watch Aunt Estie had always coveted . . . or a mandolin like the one Lois McMahon had shown off last spring at school . . . or even a gramophone! Mellie shook her head. What ever must doctors and hospitals cost? she wondered. Carefully, she put the money back into the purse.

And then she didn't know what to do with it. She ought to put it away, she thought. Put it away in some safe place against the time when Papa was home again and paying the bills.

Mellie's eyes traveled around the kitchen. They lighted on the china cupboard with its everyday dishes and—behind the stack of various-patterned plates—the black leather purse of household money. Mellie put her head to one side and considered. The unlocked, glass-paned doors of the china cupboard seemed too flimsy, the stack of plates insufficient camouflage for so great a sum of money. Mentally, Mellie walked through the house, looking for safe hiding places. The purse was too lumpy to secrete between the pages of the Bible on the library table. It was apt to get lost in the woodbin. It was too big for the sugar bowl on the dining room buffet. There was only one place Mellie could think of—Papa's desk. Papa's desk had a drawer that locked with a small brass key. Mellie had watched him open it the time he showed her the locket that had once belonged to Frances and that would someday be hers.

It was the time he found Mellie crying on the kitchen steps because the children at school had teased her. "I care for you like you *was* my own," he had said, and he had taken her to his room, the big bedroom at the back of the house where Mellie was seldom allowed. He had gone to the closet and reached up high on a shelf for the little brass key and then he had gone to the desk and unlocked the drawer.

Mellie had stood, uncertain, in the middle of the room.

"Here," Papa had said, turning from the desk when he had shut the drawer again. "Here. This was Frances's— your mama's—and someday it will be yours, when you are old enough."

Mellie had walked forward unsteadily to view the

tiny locket, heart-shaped and gold-chained, on the palm of his hand.

"She wanted you to have it," he said, "to show you she felt like you was her own little girl. She wanted . . ." Mellie remembered how Papa's voice had stopped, like he had something caught in his throat, and how his fingers had closed over the locket as he turned from her. "*You* got no call to be cryin'," Papa had said, his voice sounding angry. "There's no shame in bein' wanted as much as your mama wanted you. Now go play."

Mellie had fled, so relieved to be free of the tight, scary feeling of Papa's room that she *had* stopped crying about being adopted. She did not ever cry about it again. . . where Papa could see. But she remembered the locket, and what Papa had said about Frances, and though she had rarely been in his room from that day to this, except to clean or change the bed, she remembered the little locked drawer.

Mellie picked up the purse and the painted tin lamp. Papa's desk drawer was the very place. Even Papa would think so, she told herself. It was important not to lose so much money and—I *would* like to see the locket again, Mellie thought.

Walking through the darkened house was scary, even though the lamp shed a wavering puddle of light in which to step. The floor creaked in unaccustomed places. The sitting room chairs leaped out to trip her.

Even the few steps it took to cross the hall seemed farther than usual.

In front of Papa's closed door, Mellie paused. It felt wrong somehow to be going into Papa's room with him in the hospital. That's silly, Mellie told herself. I changed the bed in there only last Monday. It's the only place I can think of to hide the money, the best place, Mellie thought, and I'll only look at the locket for a moment or so. Papa wouldn't mind. I don't *think* he would mind . . .

Still, her hand shook when she reached out to turn the glass doorknob. She held the lamp high as she stepped over the threshold of Papa's room, and was startled by the sight of her own face—her eyes were too bright and big—in the mirror over the dresser. Heart thumping, she turned her eyes to follow the wavering light as it played over the polished wood of the dresser top, the neat blue coverlet on the old-fashioned four-poster bed—not slept in since she made it on Monday, she thought with a pang—over the nightstand—bare except for Papa's spectacles in their leather case—and the straight-backed chair and the desk beneath the window. Mellie took another step. The room was stuffy from being closed up, and it smelled of Papa, of clean denim and machine oil and cigarette smoke. Suddenly, Mellie's throat was closing with the hard pain that signaled tears. Oh, Papa! she thought.

She ran to the closet. The kerosene in the lamp was sloshing dangerously as she yanked open the door. She put the lamp on the closet floor and glanced up to the shelf. It was not as high as she remembered, but she could not reach it unaided. She dragged the desk chair into the closet and climbed onto it.

Mellie's fingers slid along the shadowed shelf, feeling around Papa's bowler hat box and along the spines of a neat row of household ledgers. Nothing. Perhaps Papa had changed the hiding place of the desk drawer key. Mellie climbed down and moved the chair farther into the closet. This time, when she ran her hand over the surface of the shelf, her fingers encountered a small tin box. She took it down and held it low so the lamplight illuminated its lid. "Dr. Wilden's Quickcure Stomach Remedy," Mellie read. Was the key inside? She snapped open the box. Nothing but pills, small pink pills. Mellie replaced the tin thoughtfully. Was this why sometimes, right after supper, Papa went to his room? To take his medicine? He had never complained of stomach trouble. But then Papa never complained of any . . .

Something cold and metallic was beneath Mellie's searching fingers. Ah! she sighed, and her fingers closed around a small brass key.

Mellie's heart was skipping with excitement as she replaced the chair in front of Papa's desk. She carried the lamp out of the closet and set it on the green paper blotter on the desk top. Then she pulled Mr. Harrison's purse out of her apron pocket.

I'll put it away in the drawer and look at the locket for just a minute, and then I'll lock the drawer up again and put away the key, she thought as she perched on the edge of the chair and turned the key in the lock of the small middle drawer.

The key turned easily.

Maybe I'll just try the locket on, Mellie thought. Just for a minute. Just to see in the mirror how it looks. Surely Papa wouldn't mind that.

She pulled open the drawer.

At first, Mellie didn't see the locket. The drawer seemed to be full of papers, folded neatly and fastened with an elastic band. She moved them aside, the lamp-light catching a glint of gold. There it was—the locket, small and heart-shaped on a thin gold chain. It nestled in the bottom of the drawer with two smooth rings of polished green glass. Mellie picked up the locket, and as she did so, the glass rings clinked together with a faint, ringing sound. Her heart stopped. She knew that sound. It was . . . It was the sound of . . .

Mellie took up the shining rings and held them in her hand, feeling their smoothness and the way they warmed to her skin. They were bracelets, she thought, and suddenly Mellie had a vision of green bracelets on a slim, tan wrist. Oi-Lin's wrist. Mellie could remember the way Oi-Lin had helped her to hold her bowl and eating sticks, and she remembered what she had not even noticed then—Oi-Lin's green bracelets and the faint, ringing sound they made when they touched. These bracelets Mellie held in her hand were much like Oi-Lin's.

Papa had said the locket was to be hers someday, a gift from her mama, Frances. Were these bracelets also Mellie's? And the papers? Were they about her?

Mellie slipped the elastic band from the papers. She knew as she unfolded them that Papa certainly wouldn't want her to see them or he would not have locked them away in the drawer.

But they are about me, Mellie thought, suddenly knowing it. They are about who I am and where I came from. They are about my real mother! Even though Papa didn't want it, she had to know what they said.

Mellie held the papers to the light and read. The top paper was a legal document. "Permission to Adopt," it was headed.

"In the matter of the guardianship of Jane Doe, also known as Liu Mei-Li . . ." Mellie read swiftly, her eyes skipping the stiff legal words. ". . . a minor child, dependent of the Boys and Girls Aid Society of Portland, Oregon . . . place and date of birth unknown, was found to be abandoned by her parents. . . ."

Abandoned.

Mellie felt the word like a stone in the pit of her stomach. She closed her eyes, waiting until she could feel her heartbeat and hear the sound of her breath drawn shakily in, and then she opened them and continued to read. She clutched the edge of the papers as though holding a lifeline.

". . . that William T. and Frances E. Langford, husband and wife, residing in the County of Multnomah, State of Oregon, are desirous of legally adopting the said child and of naming the child Mary Elizabeth Langford."

Mary Elizabeth Langford. Mellie read her own name, moving her lips silently over the familiar shape of the syllables.

But they've always called me "Mellie," she thought.

Her eyes jumped once again to the name of the abandoned child, place and date of birth unknown. "Jane Doe, also known as Liu Mei-Li."

Jane Doe was a name lawyers called you if they didn't know your name, but what was Liu Mei-Li? It looked like a Chinese name, Mellie thought.

Abruptly she pushed back the chair, snatched up the lamp, and ran to the dresser. She stood on tiptoe, face thrust close to the mirror, and studied herself.

Round blue eyes, feverish looking.

Skin so fair it blotched red and white.

Nose a little too thin.

Mouth a little too large.

Mouse-brown hair.

Not at all like Oi-Lin. Not at all like any of the black-haired, almond-eyed Chinese she had seen in Chinatown.

Mellie's heart was racing. She put her hand on it to slow it down. Of course, *she* was not Chinese.

But then, who was Liu Mei-Li?

Thursday, Going Back

Mellie sat on the front steps, waiting for Geem-Wah. She had been waiting a long time. Ever since breakfast, which she couldn't swallow, she had been sitting on the steps, her knees pressed tightly together, her fingers touching now and again the heart-shaped locket at her throat, the green glass bracelets on her wrist. Papa would be furious that she had taken them, Mellie thought, and Aunt Estie would think her gaudy, but their smoothness and shine made her feel stronger somehow, and safe. I reckon I'm just bad, she thought, but they are *mine*, whether Papa means me to have them or not. I just know they are mine.

Mellie had watched as Mr. Tilzer, across the street, came out of his house, settling his straw hat on his bald, pink head. Mr. Tilzer had worn a mail-order suit to work since he started in the timber office. "Coming up in the world," Aunt Estie had observed. "Too grand for the likes of us," said Papa. But Mr. Tilzer tipped his straw hat politely to Mellie when he saw her sitting on the steps. "Out early this morning, Mellie," he said pleasantly, and "Fine day!" before he strode briskly away to the streetcar stop.

One by one, the doors of the houses had opened and the men had come out. Some rode past on bicycles, like Papa. Some walked to the streetcar, like Mr. Tilzer. Mr. Farraday drove by in his trap. Last of all came Miss Florian, who worked at Olds, Wortman & King. "I don't have to live here, Brother," Aunt Estie declared from time to time when she was miffed with Papa. "I can always hire out as a milliner like Joanna Florian." Mellie didn't like it when Aunt Estie said things like that. "You wouldn't really?" she had asked Aunt Estie once. "You wouldn't *really* leave us?" Aunt Estie's angry face had softened, and her hand had fluttered out to pat Mellie's hand. "Oh, I suppose not," she had said. "Not so long as I'm *needed* here."

Mellie sat on the steps and fingered the locket and watched Mrs. Henry shake a rug over her porch banister. She watched old Mrs. Florian, the milliner's mother, sweep her walk. She saw Howard Tilzer come from his backyard, carrying a sack of chicken feed, and that reminded her to feed Papa's chickens. But she hurried through the job, dumping the feed in handfuls instead of scattering it evenly the way Papa liked. She ran back to the front steps, heart pounding, when she heard the sound of creaking wheels, but it was only the vegetable man. "Fresh peas, carrots, fresh-picked asparagus?" he called. Mellie shook her head and plunked down on the steps again. Where *was* Geem-Wah? Why *didn't* he come to check on her?

Ever since Mellie had found the papers last night, the papers headed "Permission to Adopt," she had known she had to talk to Geem-Wah.

He knows something, something about me, she had decided when her thoughts began to move again. He knows, and that is why he has been so kind.

She had thought it all out very carefully. She could not have asked Papa, even if he were well. Papa would have told her before this if he had wanted her to know.

But I *need* to know where I came from, Mellie thought. I need to know about my true mother. I need to know . . . who I am.

It has something to do with Geem-Wah. It has something to do with the sound of green glass bracelets ringing together—Mellie shook her wrist, listening for the soft, ringing sound—and something to do with the light and the taste and the touch and the song of my dream. It has something to do with Oi-Lin's eyes and their dark, frightened look. Mellie had to press her lips hard together to keep them from trembling. It has something to do with my nightmare, she thought.

Why *didn't* Geem-Wah come?

Two boys loped up the sidewalk and hollered for Howard Tilzer. The little boy next door came out to play with his cat.

Mellie stared down the street until her eyes ached.

Her heart thumped every time a wagon or buggy came into view.

"Hullo, Mellie. Whatcha doin'?"

Mellie jumped, startled. Lois McMahon and Clara Thom had paused in front of Mellie's house. They must have come from the other direction. They were holding hands.

"Nothing," said Mellie.

"Oh," said Lois McMahon. "Well, we're going downtown. Shopping. By ourselves."

Mellie tried to concentrate on what Lois was saying. A week ago, she would have been thrilled to have Lois stop to talk to her. But now, it somehow didn't seem important. "That's nice," Mellie forced herself to say. "Have a good time."

"Yes. Well . . . we will," said Lois, looking puzzled. "Won't we, Clara? We'll have a lovely time."

Clara nodded, looking from Lois to Mellie and back again.

"Ta ta," said Lois, fluttering her hand.

Clara giggled, and the two girls walked on.

" 'Bye," said Mellie absently, peering past them down the street.

Lois and Clara were whispering together as they walked away, and once Lois glanced back at Mellie. Probably talking about me, Mellie thought, but it didn't matter. She had more urgent concerns than Lois McMahon.

Where *was* Geem-Wah?

Suddenly, Mellie couldn't sit still another moment. She jumped to her feet and began to pace up and down the porch.

It had been evening when she had seen Geem-Wah's cart go by yesterday. Perhaps he won't come until evening today, she thought. I can't just sit and wait all day. She glanced down the street and saw Lois and Clara disappearing around the corner on their way to the streetcar stop.

The streetcar stop. They were taking the streetcar downtown.

I can do that, Mellie thought. I can take the streetcar to Chinatown and find Geem-Wah myself. I don't have to just *wait*.

But almost immediately, the smothery feeling of fear took hold of her. By myself? she thought. All by myself?

Mellie had never been downtown by herself—only with Aunt Estie shopping, and once with Papa to a vaudeville matinee. And, of course, never to Chinatown. No one went to Chinatown!

Mellie's heart was beating fast, and her dress was wet under the arms. She made herself sit back down on the steps.

What if I didn't get off the streetcar at the right stop? she thought. What if I got lost? What if I couldn't find the laundry, or I did and Geem-Wah wasn't there? What if . . .

Mellie bit her lip. She stared desperately down the street. The air shimmered and the street seemed to move, like water, before her eyes. It was empty. No one in sight. No men going to work. No children playing. No wagon or buggy or cart. No Geem-Wah.

Mellie swallowed hard and stared at her hands, twisting in her lap. The soft, green shine of the bracelets made her wrist look thin and strong. Lois McMahon and Clara were taking the streetcar downtown by themselves. If Lois McMahon can do it, Mellie thought, lifting her head, I can do it, too. I'm no baby. I'll be eleven soon. She felt as if she wanted to cry. It's better than waiting, she thought. It's better than sitting here.

"Here, please," Mellie said, her voice sounding thin and shaky. "I want to get off here."

She was glad Lois and Clara had gone ahead on an earlier car. She would not have wanted them to see where she was getting off. She thought the conductor looked at her strangely as she made her way to the door and climbed down the steps to the street. It was the first stop after they had crossed the Burnside Bridge, and Mellie knew Chinatown was near the riverfront, but she had not dared tell the conductor where she was going and ask if this was the right stop.

The streetcar clanged away. Mellie stood on the corner and looked about her fearfully. This was nothing like the neighborhood Geem-Wah had taken her to. Burly-looking men lounged in the open door of a saloon a few doors down. They were none too clean, some of them, and needing shaves. Mellie saw a woman with yellow hair sitting in a window across the street. She realized with a start that the woman wasn't a lady. For one thing, her lips were rouged. For another, she wore a flowered wrapper, and this was the middle of the day. Aunt Estie would be scandalized, Mellie thought. It was then that she saw the Chinese man.

It was not *her* Chinaman. Not Geem-Wah. But a Chinaman was apt to be going to Chinatown, and on impulse, she began to follow him.

This was a most peculiar place, Mellie thought as she hurried after the man. All sorts of odd-looking people went in and out of the ramshackle buildings. All sorts of smells—fishy smells and oily smells and even sewer smells—assaulted her nose. Voices shouted, and Mellie suspected she was hearing words of which Aunt Estie would not have approved. In the sunlight, the shrinking puddles, even the dirty windows, glinted. Mellie caught sight of a sign hanging on a bracket over the sidewalk. It was inscribed with the curling Chinese characters she remembered from her visit to Geem-Wah's. Then she saw a storefront, draped with scarlet banners. She followed the Chinese man around a corner and almost fell over a crate of quacking ducks.

Ahead of her stretched a street of brick-fronted buildings, hung with wrought-iron balconies. The sounds of the voices were suddenly different in rhythm and pitch, and the smells were the strange-familiar ones she remembered. Color shimmered from every window and door and from the clothes of the few children playing in the street.

Chinatown.

She had done it. She had taken the streetcar and used her head, as Papa was always urging, and found her way to Chinatown all by herself.

Mellie took a deep, satisfied breath. Now to find Geem-Wah!

Searching

Geem-Wah's room had been above the laundry, Mellie remembered as she walked along the crowded street. A laundry in an alley behind a high, wooden gate. There had been a shop in the building next to the alley. A shop with vegetables and eggs, and some sort of chickens hung outside, and baskets of things on the sidewalk and . . .

Mellie was staring at the Chinatown street stretching before her, staring at building after brick building with shops opening to the sidewalk beneath second-story balconies. All of the shops, it seemed to Mellie, were hung with vegetables and egg baskets and plucked, oiled birds. All had containers of fruits and vegetables set out on the sidewalk. All looked just alike!

Mellie's heart sank. I'll never find him, she thought. Never in a million years. Aunt Estie often said she hadn't a lick of sense and, stopping in her tracks to gaze in dismay, Mellie thought Aunt Estie was right. I *wasn't* using my head, she thought. I was dreaming again. Dreaming and imagining I could do something right.

Could find Geem-Wah and ask him about the name on the adoption papers and find out . . .

What? Mellie thought. I already know. A "minor child" without even a proper name, just Jane Doe, the name lawyers gave to girls who hadn't any name . . . girls "abandoned by their parents."

Mellie put out her hand to touch the cool bricks of the wall next to her. She wanted to cry, but strangely, she couldn't do even that. Her mind was stuck on that terrible word, abandoned. Parents didn't just abandon their children unless . . . unless they didn't love them. Mellie knew she had known that always, knew that it was what made being adopted so dreadful. It meant your true mother and father didn't love you, didn't want you, had *abandoned* you. . . .

Mellie realized she was being stared at. A group of men who had been talking together in the doorway of the nearest shop had fallen silent and were looking at her. Three little boys who had been trailing sticks through the mud of a drying puddle gaped with open mouths and wide black eyes.

Mellie felt her face go hot. Her own eyes fell, unable to meet the stares. She turned and stumbled back the way she had come, away from the black, hostile eyes of Chinatown. The wooden sidewalk blurred beneath her feet, her feet that went faster and faster away from the stares. The tears were coming now, as fast as her feet.

She ran across the street. Mud splashed on her stockings and into one shoe.

Someone was on the corner. She turned and ran across another street. Her hat came off and flapped against her back, held by its elastic band. Her feet thudded against the planks of the sidewalk, thudded with her racing heart. A wagon blocked her path. She tripped on a loose board and fell, tearing her stocking, and then she was up again, turning another corner and another, stumbling around a stack of crates, dodging a man in blue trousers, crossing another street.

Mellie's breath sobbed in her throat. The sun pounded on her bare head. Bit by bit, her eyes cleared and her steps slowed. Blinking, she looked to see where she was, and once more, all around her were Chinese people and balconied brick buildings and the sights and sounds and smells of Chinatown.

A woman—the first woman Mellie had seen on the street in Chinatown—was walking toward Mellie with tiny, painful, mincing steps, leaning against the two children who flanked her. The boy was as tall as Mellie and was dressed in blue trousers like his mother. The girl was smaller, her clothes rainbow-hued. All three looked curiously at Mellie, and Mellie stared back. Then the woman smiled.

From a balcony, someone called, and the woman looked up and answered, pausing in her labored progress. The soft, singing sound of her speaking stilled Mellie's heart. Mellie's eyes met the woman's eyes, and her lips curved tentatively to meet the woman's smile. The woman spoke to her.

Mellie could not understand the words, but she understood the tone. It was questioning and concerned.

"I . . . I'm looking for Geem-Wah," Mellie said. "Geem-Wah or Oi-Lin or . . . or even Mrs. Liu Tai."

"Liu Geem-Wah?" the boy said. "Are you looking for Liu Geem-Wah?"

"I don't know," Mellie said, startled to hear him speak English so well, as she had been startled the first time Geem-Wah spoke to her in her own language. "He . . . he's a laundryman. Geem-Wah, the laundryman."

"Ah, yes." The boy nodded and spoke rapidly to the woman, whose kindly face broke once more into smiles and who also nodded again and again as she answered him.

The boy turned back to Mellie. "I must help my mother to walk to that shop," he said, pointing to a store three doors down. "If you will wait, I will take you to the house of Liu Geem-Wah."

"Thank you," said Mellie, moving aside so the three could pass. As they moved slowly down the sidewalk, she looked closely at the woman's feet beneath the wide blue legs of her trousers. They looked like little stumps in tiny black satin shoes. A child's shoes, from the size of them, but on a grown-up woman. Mellie tried hard to catch hold of a memory of someone else who had feet like these. Someone she had known a long time ago . . .

Men, lounging in doorways or walking past, glanced at Mellie and talked among themselves, but suddenly they didn't seem unfriendly to Mellie. Only curious. As curious as I would be if I saw a Chinese girl on *my* street, Mellie thought. She remembered with blushing shame the taunts of the schoolchildren when the laundry cart drove by.

Mellie became aware that her knee was hurting and, pulling up her skirt a little, she looked at it. Her torn stocking was bloody and blobbed with drying mud. When Mellie saw how badly her knee was scraped, she realized it was throbbing. It needed to be washed, as Aunt Estie would have washed it, clucking her tongue and scolding Mellie for being so unladylike as to run pell-mell down a public street. It needed to be painted with iodine—no matter the sting, the sting made it better, Aunt Estie said—and bandaged with gentle hands. But there was no one there to wash and scold and soothe the hurt. Mellie felt sore and resentful as she pulled her handkerchief from her pinafore pocket and, looking about for water and seeing none, she wet a corner in her mouth and bent over to dab at the wound.

"I will take you to Liu Geem-Wah," she suddenly heard the boy saying.

Mellie gave up her futile attempt at doctoring and followed him, limping, back the way she had come.

*   *   *

The gate to the alley stood open. In daylight, the alley did not seem so menacing as Mellie remembered. She noticed there was a little garden growing at its end, under the torch bracket. An old man was watering the garden with a tin bucket of soapy water, the way Aunt Estie watered their garden with the dirty dish and laundry water. The rich, familiar smell of damp earth rose to meet Mellie's nose, blended with the laundry smells and the sounds of the men working and talking in the laundry beyond the open door.

The boy poked his head inside the door and called. A man appeared, frowning at the sight of Mellie. Mellie found herself suddenly conscious of her hat, dangling against her back, and her sweaty dress and torn stocking and bloody, muddy knee as the boy pointed to her and talked to the man, who was regarding her sullenly.

Mellie pulled at her dress and put her hat back on, tucking the wisps of her hair under it as best she could. There was nothing she could do about her knee.

"You may go in," the boy said politely, turning to her. "Through the laundry and . . ."

"Thank you," said Mellie. "I know the way." She gave one last tug to her skirt, hoping her petticoat didn't show, and squared her shoulders.

No one will hurt me, she told herself. This boy has been kind to show me the way.

She wished she had some money to give the boy, but there was only a streetcar token in her pocket. Then it occurred to her that he might be insulted if she offered him money, so she stuck out her hand to shake. The boy flashed her such a smile as he shook her hand that Mellie felt warmed clear through. He turned and ran back down the alley.

Strengthened by that smile, Mellie turned to face the frowning man at the laundry door.

Through the open doorway of Geem-Wah's room, Mellie could see Liu Tai and another tiny, old Chinese woman sitting beside a small, low table. They were talking at a great rate, their voices loud, while their small, wrinkled hands stitched busily at the mending in their laps. Liu Tai was cackling happily, her sharp black eyes almost lost in the crinkling of her laughter.

Mellie tapped softly on the open wooden door, but the old women did not hear her. She pushed the door farther open and stepped across the threshold.

"Ai-yah!" The other old woman had caught sight of Mellie and cried out, consternation on her moon-shaped face. She pointed, and Liu Tai swung around to stare. For a moment they fell silent.

"Excuse me," Mellie whispered, the words sticking in her throat. Then, more loudly, "Excuse me, I am looking for Geem-Wah."

Liu Tai dropped her mending and reached for a pair of scissors, lying on the table. She flourished them in Mellie's direction and shrieked.

Mellie retreated a step or two. "Please," she stammered. "Please, where is Geem-Wah?"

A movement in the corner caught Mellie's eye. Oi-Lin was rising from the bed where she had been sitting out of Mellie's view. Mellie turned toward her.

"Please, Oi-Lin," she said over the shrill sound of Liu Tai's voice. "Please, where may I find Geem-Wah?"

Liu Tai had scrambled to her feet. The other old woman sat as though frozen, her face shocked. Liu Tai shrilled at Oi-Lin, who had started toward Mellie. Rushing around the table, Liu Tai screamed at Mellie, her face quivering with alarm.

Mellie retreated before the assault of the old woman's voice, stumbling backward over the threshold and into the hall.

Liu Tai slammed the door in her face.

III

THE
GOWN

Betsy Forrest, Eleven Years Before

Her hand trembled so that the words wobbled across the paper in blotched and wavery lines. She couldn't make sense of them, and she didn't try. She concentrated only on their steady progression as the old Chinaman dictated them in his strange, sing-songy voice. The words had nothing to do with her, she thought—except that sometimes he asked her to supply one.

"What day?" he urged, and she searched her memory for a date.

"What time?"

I, she wrote, and the next was easy, her name and the name of the city, this hated place she must leave, could leave this very afternoon . . . as soon as she finished the writing. As soon as she finished . . . She could go directly to the station to catch the evening train home. Home.

. . . do hereby relinquish, she wrote. What a queer word, relinquish. Where had he, a foreigner, learned such a word? She would never have used it, left to herself. Give up, give away . . . Her mind veered from the word, sell.

The baby was beginning to fuss.

Don't, she thought. Please don't. Please stay asleep. Don't open your eyes, she thought. Don't look at me.

She kept her own eyes fixed on the words that formed beneath her pen point. . . . take good care, *she wrote, and those words made her feel better.*

He has promised, she thought, has promised . . .

. . . to educate her, *she wrote, as he dictated the words.*

She was coming to the end of it, and the words sounded legal and proper. Witness my hand and seal this, the 2nd day of September, A.D. 1897.

"Sign," the old Chinaman was saying, and she signed her name, this time dredging it from her memory as though it belonged to someone else, as indeed it did. It belonged to that silly girl who had come to Portland more than a year ago, her head full of dreams. A silly little girl, who believed any sweet, false words a good-looking man might whisper in her ear. Where was that girl now, she wondered, her head bowed over the paper.

The old Chinaman's hand was reaching for it. What a funny yellow hand it was. He lifted the paper from the table and breathed on it to dry the ink. His breath smelled strange, but not unpleasant. A Chinaman's breath, she thought, and her mind filled with a vision of the scene on a china plate—a weeping willow tree and two tiny, foreign figures crossing a graceful bridge to a pagoda in the distance. An alien scene all in blue and white.

"They won't hurt her?" she said, suddenly terrified at what she was doing. "You promised they will take care of her."

"They take good care," he said, and his lips curved in

what was either a smile or a leer. His eyes seemed very black and hard. "No worry," he said, and it took her a moment to understand what he said. "They take good care," he repeated.

He was handing the train ticket to her. She took it and put it carefully into her bag. Then the money. She took it from his hand and started to stuff it into the bag with the ticket.

"Count," he commanded.

Obediently, she counted the bills. She nodded. Thirty-five. There were thirty-five dollars, as they had agreed. More money than she had ever had at one time. Pa would think her time in the city well spent, when she gave it to him. "See, Pa," she would say, "I told you I would make my fortune in Portland. They pay good wages, and it was honest work."

Honest work. Could she say that, she wondered, without her tongue withering in her mouth?

She realized suddenly that the baby was screaming. Still, she did not look at her. She rose hastily from her chair.

"Well then," she said. "Is that all?"

"All," he said. "Good-bye," and he held out that strange yellow hand.

But she turned away and hurried, stumbling, to the door.

He was moving toward the basket in the corner where the baby lay, dressed in the little gown she had sewn for her, each perfect stitch her heart's speaking. He was going to pick up the baby, she knew, and she knew she couldn't bear to see those yellow hands against the filmy white lawn and lace of the gown.

She wrenched open the door and fled the crying of her baby. . . .

Oi-Lin

Mellie was trembling, trembling so hard she could scarcely stand. Behind the closed door, she heard Liu Tai's agitated voice and chairs scraping and footsteps padding on the wooden floor.

She had not expected to be welcomed with open arms to Geem-Wah's home, but she also had not expected . . . this. She put up her hand and rubbed her forehead. Her head was aching again, the way it had ached the day she stayed in bed. She drew in a long, shaky breath and turned away from the door. Well, that was that, she thought. Geem-Wah was not at home, and she did not know where else to find him. He was probably out in his cart, making his rounds. She should have known that was where he would be. Maybe driving by to see if Mellie was all right. I won't even be home, Mellie thought. If only I had stayed home and waited. Sooner or later, he'd have been sure to come by.

Mellie dragged herself to the head of the stairs and looked down. Behind her, the noise in Geem-Wah's room

was abating. Beneath her, in the laundry, she could hear
the workers and the slapping and sloshing of the wash-
tubs and the hissing of the irons.

There's nothing for it but to go home again, Mellie
thought, but instead she sank down on the step.

She was so tired, so shaky and weak. She remembered her uneaten breakfast. What time was it? Surely
past noon. Much past noon, and she had not eaten lunch
either.

Someone should be seeing that I eat, she thought.

She rested her head against the wall of the stairwell
and closed her eyes.

I'll just rest a minute, she thought, unable to face
walking once more past the hostile eyes of the laundry-
men. I'll just rest a minute until I feel stronger, and then
I'll go home and have something to eat.

She opened her eyes again at the touch on her shoulder. Oi-Lin was leaning over her, gesturing. Follow me,
she seemed to be saying, and without question Mellie
rose and followed her, away from the stairs and the door
to Geem-Wah's room. They were crossing the dim, stuffy
landing to another door, which Oi-Lin opened softly.
Light flooded through the doorway, and fresh, clean air.
Mellie stumbled into it, breathing deeply, feeling the
warm breeze on her face as her eyes adjusted to the light
of outdoors.

She and Oi-Lin were on a balcony like the ones she

had seen from the street, but this balcony overhung the back of the building. It looked out on other buildings and laundry-hung balconies and a small, grassless yard where a man was working, digging up the dirt. Mellie blinked—like a chicken in the lantern light, she thought—feeling stupid and fogged.

"What . . ." she said. "Where . . . Why . . ."

Oi-Lin put a finger to her lips and pulled on Mellie's arm to show her where to sit on the floor of the balcony. "If we are quiet here," she said softly, "no one will bother us."

Mellie sank down, rubbing her forehead, then pulled off her hat and fanned herself with it. Perhaps if she were cooler, she could think.

"You are hurt," Oi-Lin said, pointing to Mellie's knee. Mellie pulled up her skirt and examined her knee. It really did look ugly and was hurting a good deal. "Wait," said Oi-Lin, and she disappeared back into the building.

Mellie sat on the shaded balcony and tried to compose herself. Why had Oi-Lin brought her out here? The first time Mellie had come, Oi-Lin had been as frightened of her as Mrs. Liu Tai. Yes, frightened. That was what Mrs. Liu Tai was. Frightened, and not truly *angry*, as she seemed. Mellie remembered the encounter with that vulgar, threatening man the night Geem-Wah took her home in his cart, and the way all the time they were hunting for Papa, she and Geem-Wah had pretended they were not together. Because white people and Chinese did not go about together or terrible things happened to them—to the Chinese at least. I really have been thoughtless to come here and put them in danger, Mellie thought. No wonder Mrs. Liu Tai behaved that way. No wonder Oi-Lin looked so frightened that first visit. The wonder was that Geem-Wah had not been frightened, or at least that he had helped her even if he was. The wonder was that Oi-Lin did not seem to be frightened now.

Oi-Lin slipped back out onto the balcony, carrying a basin of water and a clean, white towel. She knelt before Mellie, setting down the basin, and opened the towel, which was folded into a lumpy package. In it was a little jar with a glass stopper and some strips of white cloth and an ivory comb and another, smaller towel. Oi-Lin set about wetting the small towel in the water. She handed it to Mellie.

"For washing," she said.

Mellie realized with a start how terribly dirty and sweaty she was. She blushed and began to wash her face and neck and hands while Oi-Lin rolled down the torn stocking, being careful to go gently over the scraped place on Mellie's knee.

"Why are you being so nice to me?" Mellie asked. "Aren't you scared to have me here?"

Oi-Lin looked up from bathing the knee. "You are

hurt," she said simply, as though that explained it. "You have been crying." She touched Mellie's tear-stained cheek.

"I got scared, too," Mellie admitted. "I got scared trying to find Geem-Wah by myself, and I fell down."

Oi-Lin was smoothing salve from the little glass jar onto Mellie's knee. It felt lovely and cool and didn't sting a bit. Mellie wondered if it could possibly do any good.

"Can *you* help me find Geem-Wah?" she asked. "I just *have* to talk to him."

"Liu Geem-Wah will deliver laundry until evening," Oi-Lin said. "So sorry."

Mellie reached for the comb. "May I use this?" she said, and when Oi-Lin nodded, she said, "Yes, I should have thought of that. I wanted to talk to him so badly, I couldn't wait. I should have stayed home in case he happened by. I'm sorry I upset Mrs. Liu Tai."

Oi-Lin smiled suddenly. She put her hand over her mouth to cover her smile.

"Did I say something funny?" Mellie asked.

"So sorry," Oi-Lin said. "It sounds strange when you say 'Mrs. Liu Tai.' 'Tai' *means* 'Mrs.' in Chinese, so you are saying 'Mrs. Mrs. Liu.' "

"Oh," said Mellie, pulling the comb through her tangled hair. "Then Liu is her last name. . . ." The comb stopped halfway down a strand of hair. Mellie held onto the comb, holding her thoughts as carefully still. Something slid into place in her mind. Liu. Liu was Liu Tai's

family name. Then Liu was also Geem-Wah's family
name. Liu Geem-Wah, the boy had called him. As
though she were reading it from the adoption papers,
Mellie could see the name of the child Papa and Frances
had adopted: Jane Doe, also known as Liu Mei-Li. Liu
was the family name of that child. And Mei-Li was the
name Geem-Wah called her, Mellie. It was what he had
called her from the first. Mei-Li. Not Mellie, slightly
mispronounced, as she had thought, but Mei-Li. Liu Mei-
Li. Me, Mellie thought. *I am Liu Mei-Li.*

Slowly, Mellie drew the comb to the end of the
strand. "Oh," she said, understanding and not understanding all at once.

Oi-Lin was bandaging Mellie's knee with strips of
white cloth. She glanced up at Mellie's face and stopped.

"That is *my* name, too, isn't it?" Mellie said slowly,
holding Oi-Lin's eyes fiercely with her own. "Liu Mei-
Li is my name . . . or it was . . . it was once. . . ." She
stopped in confusion. "Why?" she said. "Why did I have
a *Chinese* name?"

She put out her arm, alongside Oi-Lin's arm. The
pale arm and the tan one were both encircled by bracelets
of green.

"Please," Mellie begged. "Tell me please. I *have* to
know."

Oi-Lin rose to her feet. She picked up the basin and
the other things, took the comb gently from Mellie's
fingers. "Wait here," she said and went away.

Some little children had come out into the yard. Absently, Mellie watched them, brushing the dried mud from her stockings as she watched. She kept her mind empty. Her eyes followed the children as they raced about the small space, getting into the digging man's way until he spoke firmly to them. Then, giggling, they hunkered down near the wall and began to play.

Mellie scooted forward to peer through the railing of the balcony. The oldest child, a little girl in an embroidered cap of mulberry and blue, was folding a piece of paper into a shape, Mellie saw. When she held it up, it had become some sort of bird. The other children laughed and reached for it.

Mellie's fingers itched for a piece of paper to fold. I can do that, she thought. I know how to fold paper birds. I used to do it a long time ago. . . .

"I think you came for this," Oi-Lin said from the doorway. "I think it belongs to you."

In her hands, Oi-Lin was holding something folded into a flat, black cloth package. She carried it to Mellie and laid it in her lap.

Mellie did not look at the package. She looked at Oi-Lin's face, trying to read its meaning. Oi-Lin was not smiling.

"You know about me, don't you?" Mellie demanded, not touching the package. "You know why Geem-Wah has been so good to me. Oi-Lin, tell me," she said. "Please tell me what you know."

Oi-Lin squatted on her heels. She would not meet Mellie's gaze.

"Please," Mellie whispered. "Please."

Oi-Lin raised her eyes, and Mellie read sympathy in them. "It is not my place to tell," Oi-Lin said. "But I know your sorrow. It is mine also. My mother sold me, as your mother sold you."

"Sold"

When the black cloth was lifted back, Mellie held in her lap a baby's gown, carefully pressed and folded. Mellie lifted it and gently shook it out. A yellowed piece of newsprint fluttered from its folds, but Mellie did not look at that. Instead, she touched the fine white edging of lace at the gown's neck and sleeves and hem. The sleeves and bodice were tiny, but the skirt was full and long. Like a christening gown, she thought. She had always wondered if she had had a christening gown. By the time Papa and Frances had her baptized, she was a big girl, four years old, too old for christening gowns.

Mellie was still carefully holding away from her thoughts that terrible word Oi-Lin had said—that word that was a thousand times worse than "abandoned." She would not think about it. Instead, she would look at this little dress, which Oi-Lin claimed was hers. She smoothed its tucks and examined the tiny stitches, and then she began to fold it again. When she reached for the piece of paper to tuck back into it, she could no longer avoid seeing that it was a newspaper clipping, ragged around the edges and soft, as though it had been looked at, fingered often. The word leapt out at her.

SOLD.

Scarcely breathing, Mellie began to read.

THE OREGONIAN
WEDNESDAY, MARCH 24, 1901

ANOTHER CHILD RESCUED

WAS SOLD BY ITS MOTHER TO A CHINAMAN

Price Paid Was $35 and a
Ticket to Corvallis—
Police Take Forcible
Possession of
Youngster

A 3½-year-old girl belonging to a woman named Betsy Forrest was rescued from a Chinese joint on Second Street between Stark and Oak yesterday forenoon by Officer Shafer of the Boys and Girls Aid Society, and Detectives Page and Merrick. The Chinaman who runs the place, and in whose custody the child was, answers to the name of Liu. . . .

The words scuttled before Mellie's eyes like insects. She shook her head, trying to focus, but they moved and merged into blackness. . . .

"Do not fear," someone was saying. "Do not fear."

Mellie opened her eyes and saw that Oi-Lin and Liu Tai knelt beside her, offering a small bowl. "Drink a little," Oi-Lin was saying. "It will make you feel better. Drink."

"What . . ." Mellie tried to say, but Liu Tai held the bowl to her lips, and Mellie found herself sipping the dark, hot liquid and feeling its warmth and strength seep into her.

The old Chinese woman, Liu Tai's friend, was hovering near.

Liu Tai scolded, and the woman retreated, but she hung in the doorway and muttered to herself.

"I was frightened," Oi-Lin said. "You would not speak or move, and so I ran for Liu Tai. So sorry. I was not wise to distress you. But when Liu Tai saw that your soul had fled from your body, she was not angry with me. She . . ."

Liu Tai was speaking rapidly, and Mellie, looking at her face and hearing her voice, was not so certain she was not angry. The other old woman called out and gestured.

"Liu Tai wishes to know when last you had food," Oi-Lin said.

Mellie tried to think. No lunch. No breakfast. Supper last evening was the last meal she had eaten.

"Yesterday," Mellie said weakly. "But I'm not hungry, Oi-Lin. Truly. I feel a little sick. I don't want anything. Please, nothing to eat."

So it was strange how good the rice tasted and how quickly her stomach settled when they had helped Mellie back to their room and made her sit beside the open window and insisted that she eat.

The other old woman had been hustled away by Liu Tai. She had gone noisily and reluctantly, calling back over her shoulder as she went. Advice and opinions, Mellie guessed. It was odd how much she reminded Mellie of Aunt Estie's lady-friends.

Mellie felt a pang. Aunt Estie! She wondered if the postcard had come since she left the house.

Now Liu Tai moved around the room putting away the mending and directing Oi-Lin to rearrange the chairs. She muttered and exclaimed all the while, her face grim.

Mellie took a sip of tea and watched Liu Tai go to the barrel under the counter and lift off its lid. When the old woman began to dip out rice with a measure made of abalone shell, something final slid into place in Mellie's mind. She *did* know this room, she admitted. She did know that barrel and the tablet, with incense to burn before it, which was the family shrine. She did not know the names of these things, but she knew their uses and what they were. She had been here, had *lived* here once long ago, or in some place very like it. She *was* the child who was sold by its mother to a Chinaman.

Suddenly Mellie could not eat another mouthful. She put down the bowl and the eating sticks. She swayed to her feet.

"I've got to go," she said. "I've got to go home. A message might come about Papa."

But instead, she sat down again with a thump, her head reeling. She was overwhelmed with a desire to sleep. To close her eyes just for a moment. To not think.

"Rest here a little while," Oi-Lin said gently, taking her arm. She led her to a bed and helped her to lie down on it. Mellie reached to unbutton her shoes. She did not want to dirty the clean blue quilt. But the buttons were beyond her. Wordlessly, Oi-Lin helped her to take off her shoes.

"So sorry," Oi-Lin said, looking truly stricken. "I was not wise to give you the gown. I was not wise."

Somewhere quite near was a soft, ringing sound and the silken swish of something bright. She felt the breathing nearness of someone singing, a strange, familiar singing so near she had only to reach out to make the song her own. She reached . . .

She reached and opened her eyes.

The singing was not singing, but the sound of Oi-

Lin's voice, talking. Mellie stared at the low ceiling, which was blotched with damp. The meaning of Oi-Lin's words was just beyond her grasp. Oi-Lin was speaking Chinese. Then Mellie heard Geem-Wah's voice.

Mellie turned her head and saw him, hunched next to the stove, a tea bowl in his hands. The red curtain at the window was drawn tightly shut and the lamps were lit.

I have slept all afternoon, Mellie thought. Slept and dreamed all afternoon.

Mellie lifted herself on one elbow, and the rustling of the bedding made Geem-Wah and Oi-Lin and Liu Tai, who was once again stitching a piece of blue cloth, turn their heads to look at her. Mellie looked into the kind black eyes of Geem-Wah—*my* Chinaman, Mellie realized, was how she thought of him.

"Are you the man my mother sold me to?" Mellie asked.

He was not *that* man, Geem-Wah explained quietly to Mellie when she was seated with them near the stove, sipping the tea Liu Tai had given her.

"It is clear you must know the story," Geem-Wah said. "The rice has been cooked, and cannot be uncooked. You know much already. I do not know what will come of it, but it is clear you will know more.

"The man who bought you was my elder brother," Geem-Wah said. "His name was Geem-Keung, which means Strong Sword, and he was as strong and shining as his name. His wife was beautiful and good. His business, this laundry, was prosperous. His life was filled with luck, except that he had no child. His sons died in the womb. His wife was sick with weeping."

"And so he bought me," Mellie said.

"And so he bought you."

Mellie watched the flame that glowed through the cracks of the stove. It was a wonder, as warm as the day had been, that the heat felt good, but Mellie was chilled clear through.

"Why me?" she said, after a little while. "Why not a Chinese baby? Why not a little boy to replace his sons?"

"It is not so easy as that," Geem-Wah said.

As Geem-Wah told the story, Mellie began to understand. In the south of China, where the Lius came from, the people were very poor, so some young men came to America, the Mountain of Gold, to make their fortunes. Many thought they would come for just a little while, just long enough to make a lot of money working on the railroads or in the mining camps.

The father of Geem-Keung and Geem-Wah was the first of the Lius to travel to the Mountain of Gold. After many years in America, he had returned to his village to marry—Mellie looked at Liu Tai, trying to imagine her the young girl Geem-Wah said she had been when his father married her. But at home, money was still scarce.

So, after a while, old Liu had come back to America, leaving his wife and little son, Geem-Keung, behind. Ten years passed before he had saved enough to go home once again and this time, when he came back to America, he brought twelve-year-old Geem-Keung with him. Shortly after they left, his second son, Geem-Wah, was born in China.

"Why didn't he bring Liu Tai and you to America too?" Mellie wanted to know.

"American law does not allow laborers to bring their wives from China," Geem-Wah said. "Also, my mother was needed in China to care for my father's old parents. He thought that, with Geem-Keung working, too, they would soon be able to go home to China for good."

Geem-Keung had grown to manhood in America, working alongside his father. They sent so much money back to China that the old grandparents lived out their days in comfort. Geem-Wah, the younger son, was sent to school. Eventually, Geem-Keung and his father started a business in Portland, the laundry. And then the father died.

By then, Geem-Keung had lived in America for many years. He did not wish to return to China. As the owner of a business, he had a merchant's right to bring over female relatives, so, finding himself alone, he sent for his mother and brother to join him. Instead of coming herself, however, Liu Tai chose a beautiful young wife for her eldest son from among the maidens of a neighboring village and sent her, in the care of the young Geem-Wah.

"My mother said it was time that her eldest son had sons to carry on the family tradition. Lan-Heung, the girl she chose, was strong and lotus-footed and schooled in the four virtues of a woman. But after five years and three dead sons, she bore no more children."

In China, Geem-Wah explained, when a family did not have sons, they adopted them. If they needed daughters to help with women's work, or perhaps to raise as wives for their sons, they bought the daughters of poor folk, as Liu Tai had bought Oi-Lin to be her *mui-tsai*, her servant.

"But . . . but *buying* babies!" Mellie said. "I think that's wrong."

"In China, it is the custom. Families who buy babies want them and love them. Families who sell babies need the money to feed other children," Geem-Wah said.

But in America, there were few Chinese babies to be bought. Chinese women were few, far outnumbered by men, and families who had babies prized them. Sometimes, however, there were white or black or Indian babies available; not from orphanages, of course—"You see what happened when the authorities found out a white baby was being raised in a Chinese family," Geem-Wah said—but in other ways. Geem-Keung and Lan-Heung began to search for a child. At last, the old child broker told them of a baby who could be obtained for a sum of money and the price of a train ticket, but the baby was a girl.

"Me," said Mellie, turning her tea bowl around and around in her hands.

"You," said Geem-Wah.

The Rest
of the Story

In the darkness, Mellie could hear their breathing—the light, sighing breathing of Oi-Lin, the whistling snore of Liu Tai. Mellie thought she could not remember ever sleeping before in the same room with another person, much less two other people.

But I must have, she thought. In the orphanage where the police took me when they took me away, there must have been other children. And before that, I must have slept in this very room with Lan-Heung and Geem-Keung. I lived here for almost four years, Geem-Wah says. Four happy years, Geem-Wah says.

Mellie wished she could remember.

She turned over on the pallet Geem-Wah had made for her on the floor before he went to the room where he slept with the laundry workers. Oi-Lin had offered Mellie her bed, but Mellie felt odd about turning her out of her own bed. "I can sleep on the floor as well as you," she had said. "It will be an adventure."

As though I hadn't had enough adventures already, Mellie thought.

She hadn't wanted to go home. "It's too risky for you to take me," she had said to Geem-Wah. "I know that now. If I may stay the night, please, I can go home on the streetcar in the morning by myself." She felt very brave saying it, and very self-sufficient.

Geem-Wah bowed his head, thinking, but Liu Tai had spoken, questioning and then declaring something in a decided sort of tone.

Mellie had stayed.

She was glad, she realized, less because of the risk to Geem Wah averted than because she simply didn't want to go back to the empty house. Here in the Lius' room, the house and even Papa and Aunt Estie seemed far away and little to do with her. She didn't want to leave the warmth of the stove and the coziness of the lamplight and the voices and faces and nearness of the Lius.

But now she could not sleep.

I need to sort it out, she thought. This morning I didn't know anything except that Papa and Frances adopted me when I was four and that there was a Chinese name on the papers. Tonight I know . . .

Everything? Mellie wondered. Do I know everything now? And is knowing better . . . or worse? Do I really know, even now, who I am?

The newspaper clipping the Lius had saved had told a great deal. Mellie had read it carefully by the light of the lamp while Geem-Wah told her more.

The woman who gave her birth was named Betsy
Forrest. The clipping said so and quoted a bill of sale
which Geem-Keung had shown the police when he tried
to get Mellie returned to him.

Bill of sale, Mellie thought, like I was a horse . . .
or a piece of furniture!

> I, Betsy Forrest, do hereby relinquish
> and give permission to Liu Geem-Keung
> to adopt, educate and raise my girl
> baby . . .

"Why would she do that?" Mellie had wanted to
know. "How could she give me up? Didn't she like me
at all?"

Oi-Lin had spoken suddenly. "My mother sold me
to Liu Tai so I would have a better life—enough to eat
and a good place to live and training in the four virtues
for the day I will marry."

"But that's different," Mellie had said to Geem-
Wah. "In China, many people are poor. You said so
yourself. You said that was why your father came to
America, to keep the family from starving. People in
America don't starve. My mother could have kept me if
she had wanted to."

Geem-Wah looked at her.

After a little, he said, "Do you remember the county
hospital? In America, some people are poor.

"The child broker said that the young mother wept," Geem-Wah said.

Mellie had looked down at the clipping, feeling uncomfortable: ". . . raise my girl baby and take good care of her . . ." read the words of the bill of sale. Her eyes skipped to the last words of the article: "The police do not know who Betsy Forrest is."

"When you arrived at this house," Geem-Wah said, "a party was given in your honor. Well-wishers brought you lucky money, and in return, Geem-Keung gave them red-dyed eggs for good fortune. Lan-Heung smiled all day long and held you in her arms."

"*She* wanted me anyway," Mellie had said.

Now, in the middle of the night, Mellie sat up on the pallet and hugged her knees. She was sleeping—not sleeping, Mellie thought—in her shift. Oi-Lin had given her the blue quilt for a cover.

She knew now why Oi-Lin's eyes had so disturbed her the first time she saw them. It was because she was frightened, Mellie thought. I was remembering Lan-Heung's eyes, my Chinese mother's eyes, from the time the police came and took me away. Lan-Heung had been terrified, Geem-Wah said.

The clipping told about it:

> The officers went into the lower part of
> the Liu domicile, which serves as a sort
> of cheap Chinese laundry. . . .

"Cheap?" Mellie had said. "My papa thinks the laundry is very dear."

"I do not think the reporter meant it was inexpensive," Geem-Wah said. "I think he meant the laundry looked mean and shabby to him."

"Oh," said Mellie.

Five Chinamen were lolling about . . .

"I see what you mean," said Mellie.

> . . . and they seemed to guess by instinct that the two officers had come to take away the child. Liu was not there, but one Chinaman flew at Merrick's throat and was floored by a right hook on the point of the chin. . . .

"Who . . ." said Mellie, looking up at Geem-Wah. "I was knocked unconscious," Geem-Wah said.

> Page and Merrick then went upstairs. They tried to gain admittance into the living apartments of the Liu family, but Mrs. Liu refused to open the door. The warrant was read to her through the closed door . . .

"Did she understand English?" Mellie asked, and Geem-Wah shook his head.

. . . and then the detectives kicked the
door in, and took forcible possession of
the child.

Mellie had remembered her bad dream as she read.
She remembered the smell and the darkness and the
roughness of the arms holding her. She remembered the
smothery feeling and the struggle and the screaming.

"I remember," Mellie said. "Now I remember." But
why had she not remembered before this? Mellie said,
"What happened to Lan-Heung and Geem-Keung?
Where are they now?"

She knew somehow what his answer would be even
before Geem-Wah said, "So sorry, Mei-Li."

Of course, she thought, as he told her of the plague
in 1903, of how the grieving Lan-Heung had sickened
and died.

"My brother was bereft," said Geem-Wah. "He also
died within the year."

Mellie nodded.

"Did you know who I was, even before last Monday
when Papa was hurt?" she wanted to know.

"I, and Geem-Keung before me, have always known
where you were, Mei-Li, and how you fared," he said.

Now, Mellie pulled the blue quilt around her shoulders, shivering.

It was a comfort, she thought, to know that Geem-
Wah, and Geem-Keung before him, had cared enough

to watch over her all these years. It was a comfort against
the sad litany that murmured in her head:

Betsy Forrest sold me,

Lan-Heung lost me,

Frances went and died on me,

And . . . and Aunt Estie left me to go to the beach!

Mellie felt a little silly, thinking about Aunt Estie.
Going to the beach for a holiday seemed so trifling in
comparison to what Betsy Forrest had done, or what Lan-
Heung had suffered, or to the death of poor Frances.

It's not the same thing at all, Mellie tried to tell
herself.

But it *felt* the same.

She went away when I needed her, Mellie thought,
a hard, hurting lump in her throat. She went away. . . .

She's coming back, Mellie told herself, trying to
swallow the lump. Aunt Estie only went for a month.
She's coming back.

But will she come back always? Will she? Always?

She's not my mother, Mellie reminded herself. Not
like Betsy Forrest, who gave birth to me, or even Lan-
Heung and Frances, who wanted me so badly. She's my
aunt. Only my aunt, who takes care of me because she
has no place else to go, like Papa says.

It was peculiar that thinking such thoughts did not
make Mellie cry. She had spent such a great deal of time
crying these past few days, she supposed she was all cried

out. Or perhaps knowing about Geem-Wah helps, Mellie thought. Geem-Wah cares, and Papa cares, and . . .

I reckon *I* care, Mellie thought suddenly, feeling angry. I care what happens to me. When other people won't—or can't—take care of me, I'll just have to take care of myself.

For some reason, the thought and the anger warmed her. Mellie lay down on the pallet and snuggled beneath the quilt.

It's what I've *been* doing, Mellie thought. I've *been* taking care of myself since Monday. I can do it.

Still, she was glad for the sound of the others', alive and warm in the night.

Friday, Home

"I wonder why I didn't remember," Mellie said, half aloud.

She was standing at the streetcar stop on Burnside Street. Geem-Wah waited with her. Three other Chinese men stood nearby. "If a policeman comes, I will act as though I am with them," Geem-Wah had said. The men did not look directly at Mellie, but she knew they were watching her. They are curious, she thought, because I'm out of place. But she did not *feel* out of place somehow. It felt right to be standing beside Geem-Wah, waiting for the streetcar to carry her home. To my *other* home, she thought.

A person can have more than one place, she thought. A person can have more than one family. But . . .

"Why didn't I remember?" she said again out loud. "I should have remembered Lan-Heung and Geem-Keung. I should have remembered being taken away, being put in the orphanage. Why, I didn't even remember Frances very well. . . ." Her voice trailed off. "I was five years old when Frances died," Mellie said after a moment.

"That's old enough to remember."

"Sometimes it is easier to forget," Geem-Wah said, "when the memories hurt."

Even before she opened the door, Mellie knew that the house was no longer empty.

Someone is here, she thought, walking up the steps to the front porch.

The shades were still drawn, as she had left them. The door was closed. She had seen no smoke from the chimney as she came down the street from the streetcar stop. Still, something was different about the house. The bright midmorning sun reflected from its white fir siding. A robin chirped in the weeping birch. The rosebuds in the beds beside the porch were swelling, ready to burst forth in the scarlet blooms Aunt Estie loved. The house felt homey, comfortable again—not the vast echoing structure of the past few days.

Has Papa come home from the hospital? Mellie wondered, her heart lifting. She reached out to press the latch, pushed open the front door, and fairly ran over the threshold before the voices stopped her just beside the umbrella stand.

Mellie heard a shriek and saw Aunt Estie, standing transfixed in the middle of the living room.

"Mellie!" Aunt Estie cried. "Mellie Langford, where *have* you been?"

Then Aunt Estie was running to her and folding her

in her arms, and Mellie's face was pressed against her
ample, rose-water-scented bosom. Aunt Estie was crying
and talking and hugging her all at once. "Mellie Langford, you will be the death of me, the death of me once
and for all. Where *have* you been, you wicked girl. Don't
you know you had us all frightened half out of our wits,
what with Brother hurt and you turning up missing and
the neighbors not even knowing anything was wrong
and . . ."

"Let the child breathe, Ess," said Papa's voice,
sounding funny and weak.

"Papa," Mellie cried, pulling away from Aunt Estie.
"Papa, you've come home. You've woken up and come
home!"

Papa was stretched out on the living room sofa.
Around his head glared a big, white bandage, and his
eyes looked red-rimmed and swimmy. He was pulling
himself to a sitting position, and he looked very thin and
white.

"Papa, I was so worried," Mellie cried, running to
kneel beside the sofa and clasp the trembling hand he
held out to her. "They wouldn't let me see you, and they
said you were unconscious, and they wanted to put me
in an orphanage, and I thought you might die. . . ."

Mellie realized the room was full of people. Not just
Aunt Estie and Papa, but lots of people—Mrs. Henry
from across-the-alley and the whole Tilzer family, even

Howard, and Aunt Estie's lady-friends and half a dozen other neighbors.

Mellie clutched Papa's hand and looked around at their faces. "What in the world's going on?" she asked. "Why is everyone here? What's been happening while I was gone?"

Papa looked and looked at her, his eyes fierce and happy and . . . full of tears, Mellie realized with astonishment. Papa's throat was working, his Adam's apple moving convulsively, and Aunt Estie was laughing and crying, kneeling beside Mellie and touching her and talking a mile a minute, and everyone else was talking, too.

It wasn't easy to sort it out, but gradually Mellie began to understand. The day before, while she sat waiting for Geem-Wah on the front porch steps, Papa had awakened in the hospital. It had taken awhile, he said, to figure out what he was doing there. The last he had known, he was at work in the factory yard. But, when he realized how long he had been unconscious, he also realized that Mellie must be at home alone, and had been alone for several days. "I raised a ruckus," Papa said, "but all I got from them nuns was some crazy tale of a little girl who come asking for me and then run off. I made them send 'round to the house to find you."

"Only the messenger didn't find *you*, Mellie dear," Aunt Estie said. "He found me, just getting home from the beach."

"But you weren't supposed to come home for a long time yet," Mellie said. "You were going to stay for a whole month, for a whole long month of holiday."

"As if Estelle Langford *could* stay away from her family for a month," said Miss Emma Jenkins. "Five days, and she was so homesick that nothing must do but we all must pack up and head back to Portland."

"You didn't *have* to come back with me," Aunt Estie snapped. "I am perfectly capable of traveling alone. You were just as eager as I to be shut of that place."

"Well, it *was* raining," said Miss Louise.

"It just wasn't much fun without William and you," Aunt Estie said.

"So we came back early," said Miss Emma, sniffing. "And a good thing, too!"

Aunt Estie had gone straight to the hospital with the messenger. "At first I was just worried about William. I could see you had slept in your bed and fixed a bite of breakfast for yourself . . ."

"I meant to do up my dishes later," Mellie said, but Aunt Estie just waved a hand and continued.

"I thought you were off playing somewhere. Oh, I didn't know *what* to think!"

Aunt Estie had convinced the hospital that she could take care of Papa at home. "All he needs now, the doctor says, is rest and nourishment."

"I thought you were going to die, Papa," Mellie said, tears coming to her eyes now that she could admit it. "I thought you were going to die and leave me."

Papa patted her arm. "Can't do that, Mellie-girl,"
he said. "I've got you to rear and Ess here to take care
of."

"As if I can't take care of myself, and you, too, for
that matter," Aunt Estie muttered.

"But when you didn't come home last night," Papa
said, "we got perturbed."

"We got *frantic*," Aunt Estie said.

"You telling this, or am I?" said Papa.

"You are, William. Go on. Just don't tire yourself."

"Everyone's been out huntin' for you, Mellie-girl.
All these good people here. They've scoured the neighborhood." His voice was beginning to sound stern.

"She was sitting on your stoop yesterday forenoon
big as life," Mr. Tilzer said. "I saw her, and Howard
did, too."

"So where did you go to worry us so?" Papa demanded, and Mellie thought his mustache was bristling
a little, as though he were forgetting how glad he was
to see her. "Where have you been all night?"

As Mellie was trying to decide how to answer, she
heard the front door open. She raised her eyes and saw
Mr. Harrison, from Papa's work, coming into the living
room, and with him was Lois McMahon.

"Is this the girl you saw talking to Miss Mellie,
Howard?" Mr. Harrison was saying, and then he caught
sight of Mellie herself beside Papa's sofa. "Why, Miss

Mellie, they've found you," he said.

"I thought you were lost," said Lois McMahon, looking disappointed.

"No," said Mellie. "I wasn't lost. I was just . . ."

Everyone was looking at her. Mellie swallowed hard and looked down at the bracelets on her wrist. Not glass, Geem-Wah had told her, but precious jade. "We Chinese believe that circles of jade will keep us safe. Lan-Heung put tiny jade bracelets on your wrists as soon as you came into our house, and when you outgrew those baby bracelets, Geem-Keung sent for larger ones from China. But they had not yet come when the policemen took you away. So Lan-Heung put her own bracelets on you and prayed to the goddess of mercy to keep you from harm."

And I *have* kept from harm, Mellie thought now, looking at the bracelets.

"I was just . . ." Mellie said. "I was just visiting . . . in Chinatown."

Afterward

Mellie thought she had never been so quickly shushed in all her life. Suddenly, Aunt Estie was bustling about, thanking the neighbors for their help. "William has had enough excitement for one day," she was saying. "I'm sure you understand that he needs his rest."

"I'm beholden," Papa kept saying, his voice low and his eyes cast down, as the neighbors took their leave.

"Nonsense, man," Mr. Tilzer said briskly. "You'd do the same for me."

"I'm just *so* relieved she's been found," said Mrs. Henry, casting a curious glance at Mellie. "I should have realized. I'll just never forgive myself for not *realizing* the poor child was all alone."

"All's well that ends well," said Miss Emma Jenkins, her eyebrows arched significantly. "We'll call on you tomorrow, Estelle, to see what we can do."

"Rest easy now, Bill," said Mr. Harrison. "We'll be glad to see you back at work when you're better."

Aunt Estie fluttered to the door with Mr. Harrison.

"I don't know how to thank you," she kept saying. "You were *such* a tower of strength."

Mellie thought Mr. Harrison looked embarrassed. His big, florid face flushed redder, and he kept turning his cap in his hands. "Weren't nothin', Miss," he said. "Weren't nothin' a-tall."

Mr. Harrison was going to take Lois McMahon home.

"Chinatown?" Lois whispered as she sidled past Mellie to the door. "*You* spent the night in *Chinatown?*"

"Good-bye, Lois dear," Aunt Estie said firmly. "Thank you for coming."

Aunt Estie closed the door after Lois McMahon and Mr. Harrison very quickly, Mellie thought. She stood for a moment, her hand resting on the handle, looking out the oval glass of the door. Then she turned to face Mellie, leaning her back against the door. She drew a deep breath.

"And now, Mellie dear," she said. "About Chinatown . . ."

But Papa was straining off the sofa toward Mellie, his eyes flashing black. His face was blotched red and white, and his voice shook. "What was you doin' in that place?" he demanded. "Tell me now and tell me quick. What was you doin' in Chinatown?"

It was hard to find the words to tell him, with him breathing so hard in sharp, alarming gasps and searching her face with those terrible eyes. Mellie's voice stumbled, sometimes disappearing altogether in a hoarse whisper, as she tried to tell about the message coming, about Geem-Wah's kindness, about the odyssey in Geem-Wah's laundry cart to find Papa. Perhaps hardest of all was telling about finding the adoption papers and the bracelets in Papa's desk drawer.

"Oh, Mellie, my dear!" Aunt Estie said. "That was snooping!"

But Papa said nothing, only sank deeper into the sofa cushions, his face as white as the bandage on his head.

"I had to know, Papa. I just had to," Mellie whispered, "and so I went back, and they told me. They told me all about it. About how Betsy Forrest sold me. About my Chinese family . . ."

Papa reared up and clutched her arm, his eyes wild. "You ain't got no family in Chinatown," he said. "Your family's right here in this house—your aunt Estelle and me. *We're* your family, Girl. Do you understand?"

"Now, Brother, don't get overwrought," soothed Aunt Estie. "Mellie didn't mean it that way, did you, Mellie dear? This whole affair has been so unsettling, it's hard to know who's who and what's what and *that's* a fact!"

Papa fell back to the sofa, breathing hard.

Mellie's heart was pounding. She had known he wouldn't like it, wouldn't like her knowing. That's why he had kept it a secret. That's why he'd never given her the bracelets or showed her the papers. But why? Why didn't he want her to know? Because they were Chinese?

"Papa, if you *knew* them . . ." she said.

But Papa wasn't listening. "Do you, Girl?" he was saying between clenched teeth, and his fingers hurt her arm. "Do you understand?"

"You'll do yourself an injury, Brother," Aunt Estie warned, her voice sharp.

"You stay out of this, Ess. She's got to understand. I'm her father, and Frances was her mother. It's the way Frances wanted it. She wanted . . ."

Mellie watched in horror as the tears spilled over onto Papa's thin cheeks. His shoulders were shaking. He put a hand over his eyes.

"Go upstairs to your room, Mellie dear," said Aunt Estie, moving toward Papa.

"But, Papa," Mellie was saying. "But, Papa, I didn't mean . . ."

"*Now*, Mellie dear. Go to your room *now*," Aunt Estie said. "We'll talk about this later when we are calm."

Sometimes in the weeks and months that followed that strange first week of summer, Mellie thought they would never be calm again.

Not that Papa shouted at her anymore. Not that he ever cried again. But though the bandage came off his head a few days later, it was a long time before Papa's face had any color in it. His eyes stayed darkly sunken.

They followed her, Mellie thought, with a sadness that was sadder than before.

Aunt Estie was not at all subdued.

"You be good to your papa, Mellie Langford," she scolded. "And you be grateful, too. Heaven knows he works his fingers to the bone so's you'll have a nice house to live in and food to eat and pretty clothes and a happy life."

Mellie remembered what Oi-Lin had said: "My mother sold me to Liu Tai so I would have a better life." Perhaps that *is* why Betsy Forrest sold me, Mellie thought. It's what they all wanted me to have—the Lius and Papa, too.

I *should* be grateful, Mellie thought.

Aunt Estie scolded Papa, too.

"What Mellie knows, she knows, Brother," Mellie overheard her say. "She can't un-know it now."

It reminded Mellie of what Geem-Wah had said: "The rice has been cooked, and cannot be uncooked."

"I think it's just as well she knows," Aunt Estie said. "Those people took good care of Mellie. They must have felt something for her, and if it weren't that we'd not have gotten her else, I'd say it's a sad thing she was taken from them. I feel for that poor Chinese woman, I really do. And I'll tell you something else, Brother. Frances would have, too. Frances knew what it was to have no child. And then at last to be given one. I reckon Chinese folk have feelings like us. Like me and you and

Frances, poor thing. So what's *wrong* with Mellie knowing *they* loved her and wanted her, too? What's wrong with a child having lots of family? Yes, even Chinese family, if that's what she's got?"

Lots of family . . . Chinese family . . . Mellie thought about that a lot.

She thought about it so much that, when school started that fall, Mellie did something she never would have thought she'd have the courage to do. How did I dare? she thought later. But she did.

Mellie wore her jade bracelets to school.

"Why, Mellie," Lois McMahon said when she noticed them. She said it loudly, so everyone turned and looked. "Why, Mellie, where ever did you get those pretty glass bracelets? Did you get them in Chinatown that time this summer? That time you ran away?"

Mellie felt her face grow hot. She wanted to push the bracelets out of sight under her sleeve. The way Lois said "Chinatown" made it sound like a terrible place.

But I didn't hide them, Mellie thought later. I didn't slink away. It made her feel proud to remember.

"I didn't run away to Chinatown," Mellie said. "I went there visiting." She said it loudly, too, so everyone could hear.

"Visiting?" jeered Lois McMahon. "Visiting in *Chinatown?*"

"Yes, visiting," Mellie said, feeling suddenly not

embarrassed, but angry. Very, very angry. "Is there something wrong with that?"

Lois McMahon looked startled. Her voice faltered a moment. "Who . . . who . . . who in the world could you *visit* in *Chinatown?*"

"I have . . . friends in Chinatown," Mellie said. "Really sort of family. I used to live there, you know. In Chinatown. When I was a baby."

Lois's mouth was hanging open. "With Chinamen?" she squeaked.

"With Chinese people," Mellie said. "I had a Chinese mother and a Chinese father and an uncle and a grandmother, too. They gave me these bracelets. These *jade* bracelets."

Clara Thom had sidled near. She reached out to touch Mellie's bracelets.

"Truly?" she breathed. "You truly *lived* in Chinatown?"

And Mellie was surprised to see the wondering look in her eyes. The wondering, *interested* look that was usually turned to Lois McMahon.

April 1909
Pure Brightness

Mellie reached hesitantly toward Papa's hand, which swung stiffly at his side as they walked. She touched it and felt his big fingers close over hers, tightly.

"Thank you, Papa," she said in a low voice, not looking at him, but fixing her eyes instead on Aunt Estie, who swayed ahead of them beneath her parasol, arm in arm with Mr. Harrison.

Papa made a sound.

They were coming to the cemetery gate. It was old, Lone Fir Cemetery, and gone wild over the years. Mellie saw Aunt Estie gather in her skirts to keep them from brushing against the wet bushes that overgrew the path.

Papa shook his head and muttered. "Somethin' needs to be done about this place," he said. "It's a disgrace."

Many of the tombstones were overturned, and old bottles and trash littered the ground beneath the shrubbery. But Mellie knew that Frances's grave would be tidy. Papa saw to that. She clutched the flowers she had brought to put on the headstone, narcissus and white lilacs for their scent, and dainty bluebells.

"Will they be here yet?" Papa asked sharply.

"I don't know. He said about ten o'clock. We've got time to go to Mama's grave."

Mellie saw Papa's face relax a little when she called Frances "Mama." "She *was* your mother truly," he had told her, "if wanting made it so."

"I'm sure it did," said Aunt Estie. "Wanting a child is exactly what makes a woman a mother. Mellie filled that need for Frances, as she has filled it for me."

Frances's grave was at the far end of the cemetery on the north side. They walked over the long, spring green grass until Mellie spotted it beneath the weeping birch Papa had planted there. "Like the one at home," Aunt Estie said.

Aunt Estie and Mr. Harrison had come to a halt near the tree. Mr. Harrison pulled off his bowler hat and held it in his hands.

Mellie heard a sighing as Papa knelt beside the grave. He pulled a few stray shoots of grass away from the marble stone. "Beloved Wife and Mother," the headstone read.

"Here, Papa," Mellie said, holding out the flowers.

"You'll need water," Aunt Estie said.

Mellie remembered where the water spigot was. She ran off, glad of something to do, taking the little tin vase they had brought for the flowers. As she filled it, water splashed cold on her hands. Mellie felt like laughing to feel the cool water and see its dancing sparkle in the sunlight.

Papa came, she thought. He came because he loves me. She knew it, clear to her bones—knew how much Papa loved her despite his silences and gruffness. She had known ever since she saw his face that day last summer when he had thought her lost.

He'll never leave me if he can help it, she thought, just as Aunt Estie won't leave me.

Aunt Estie and Mr. Harrison were going to live next door when they were married—"So's I can keep an eye on Brother and you," she had said. Papa and Mellie would have a housekeeper, a friend of Mrs. Prucha. "I'll keep an eye on *her* too," Aunt Estie said.

The water sloshed over the lip of the vase, and Mellie turned off the spigot. She ran back to the grave, keeping a proper solemn face despite her gladsome heart.

It will be all right, she told herself. *I* shall make it right.

Aunt Estie helped Mellie and Papa arrange the flowers. Then they stood up and stepped back.

"I wish you had known Frances, Woody," Aunt Estie said to Mr. Harrison.

Papa straightened his shoulders and put on his hat.

Mellie looked into his face and touched his arm. "I remember her," Mellie said, feeling glad that she did remember now, in spite of the hurt that remembering brought.

Papa patted her hand awkwardly. He cleared his throat. "Now then, Mellie-girl," he said. "Where will they be?"

Mellie led the way to the south side of the cemetery. She could see a few Chinese people going the same way, but she did not know them. When they rounded a snarl of blackberry vines, Mellie saw several groups of Chinese clustered here and there among the graves of a section near the road. Among them, she spotted Geem-Wah, standing head and shoulders above old Liu Tai and Oi-Lin.

Mellie waved to the Lius.

"My word," Aunt Estie was fluttering. "My word, how exotic they look!"

Although she had not met them, Aunt Estie knew a great deal about the Lius. She knew that Liu Tai, as the eldest family member, had finally given permission for Mellie to visit—discreetly, so as not to bring them trouble—from time to time. "Mei-Li is the child of my eldest son's heart," Liu Tai had said. She knew that Oi-Lin had become Mellie's friend. "Geem-Wah has taught her to speak English," Mellie said, "and she likes to practice on me."

Aunt Estie had listened to Mellie tell all this, for it was Aunt Estie who had championed her when she wanted to go back to Chinatown.

Now, Geem-Wah was walking toward them. Mellie looked from his smooth tan face to Papa's. Papa's lips were white beneath his black mustache, and Mellie could see that he was looking Geem-Wah searchingly in the eye. Geem-Wah returned his gaze. Then Geem-Wah bowed deeply. "You are welcome," he said.

"I owe you a debt of gratitude," Papa said, "for helping my little girl when I was hurt last summer."

"It is not worth mentioning," said Geem-Wah. "Will you come this way?"

He led them to Liu Tai and Oi-Lin, who stood near three graves with flat, red-painted markers inscribed in Chinese.

"How do you do," Aunt Estie said, putting out her hand to Liu Tai. "You must be Mrs. Liu. Mellie has told me so much about you. I'm Estelle Langford, Mellie's aunt."

Liu Tai glared at Aunt Estie, but she bowed, keeping her hands folded inside her wide sleeves.

Aunt Estie laughed nervously. "My word," she said, and then she, too, bowed low, holding the edge of her skirt with one hand and her parasol with the other.

Mellie saw Liu Tai's eyes crinkle suddenly, and her mouth curved in a wide, toothless grin. She spoke.

"What does she say?" Aunt Estie wanted to know.

Oi-Lin ducked her head, hiding a smile. "She hopes

you have many sons, Missy," she said.

"Well, not quite yet," Aunt Estie said, flustered. She glanced at Mr. Harrison. "Not *quite* yet."

They stood then, trying not to stare at one another. Mellie's heart was racing.

Will it be all right? she wondered.

Geem-Wah turned to Liu Tai.

Liu Tai picked up a willow branch that had been placed near the markers and handed it to Oi-Lin.

Oi-Lin began to sweep the graves. Back and forth, back and forth, her arm swept. The sweeping branch made the graves smooth and clean. As Mellie watched she felt a smooth clean place being cleared in her heart as well.

Geem-Wah stepped forward and lit sticks of incense, which he stuck into the earth of the graves. Oi-Lin took from a basket small dishes of food—barbecued pork and hard-boiled eggs and rice and fruit. Geem-Wah placed the dishes on the graves. As he did so, he bowed again and again to the graves of his father, old Liu, and his brother, Geem-Keung, and his brother's wife, Lan-Heung.

Mellie's throat felt tight and sore as she watched. Though Aunt Estie had come back from the beach, and would always come back if she could, Mellie knew, nothing could bring back Lan-Heung, buried in the newly swept grave. Nothing could bring back Frances, at rest

beneath the weeping birch. And no one knew where Betsy
Forrest was, or even if she lived.

Betsy Forrest sold me,
Lan-Heung lost me,
Frances went and died on me. . . .

I surely do run through mothers, Mellie thought,
and the thought was so peculiar she found herself smiling.

Smiling, Mellie thought. Isn't it strange? I can still
smile.

Then something else occurred to her.

I suppose, she thought, in some way my mothers
have become a part of *me*. I may have Betsy Forrest's blue
eyes or brown hair, and I know that Lan-Heung is often
in my dreams, and Frances . . . Frances left me Papa and
Aunt Estie to love.

Geem-Wah and Liu Tai and Oi-Lin were bowing to
the graves. Mellie found herself stepping forward and
folding her hands in front of her. She bowed, as the Lius
were doing, first to the grave of old Liu, then to the
grave of Geem-Keung, and finally to Lan-Heung's grave.

"Slowly, walk slowly, Ma-Ma," she whispered, saying the Chinese good-bye that Oi-Lin had taught her.

I didn't have a chance to say good-bye before, she
thought.

Geem-Wah was facing Papa. "We are honored that
you have joined us in honoring our ancestors," he said.
"Pray take food with us."

Papa cleared his throat. "We should be gettin' on

home," he said. "We come because Mellie here wanted to, and because I'm beholden to you. . . ."

"Papa," Mellie said, keeping her voice polite and calm. "Please, Papa, please."

Papa looked at her. He looked at Geem-Wah. He looked at Liu Tai and Oi-Lin, standing quietly near. Suddenly he stuck out his hand to Geem-Wah. "We'd be obliged, sir," he said.

Geem-Wah shook Papa's hand.

Papa looked at Geem-Wah, and then *he* bowed.

"Little as she was, she wouldn't let us call her Mary Elizabeth, like we'd planned," he said suddenly, as though someone had asked. "So my wife said 'Mellie' would do. It was what she'd answer to."

Geem-Wah smiled. "Mei-Li," he said.

I knew then who I was, Mellie thought. Now I know again.

She looked from Geem-Wah to Papa and back again. She looked at Aunt Estie and at Mr. Harrison, who was going to be her Uncle Woody. She looked at Oi-Lin and Liu Tai.

I shouldn't have had any of them to love, she thought, if Betsy Forrest hadn't given me up.

Perhaps I'll find her, too, someday, Mellie thought. Perhaps.

The Chinese people all about them were settling down beside the graves to eat their Ching Ming feast, their feast of Pure Brightness, as Oi-Lin had called it.

"It is a day for remembering our ancestors," Oi-Lin had told Mellie, "and for remembering we owe our lives to them."

"It is certainly a fine day for a picnic," Aunt Estie was saying. Liu Tai answered her . . . in Chinese.

Mellie began to help Oi-Lin to unpack and hand around the food from the baskets the Lius had brought.

Together, they sat on the dew-damp grass and ate.

On either side of Mellie, Papa and Geem-Wah ate silently, and in the silence, Mellie could feel a sort of reaching—the way Geem-Wah had reached to grasp Papa's hand, the way Papa had reached to bow—as though they were reaching through *her*.

I will make it all right, she thought again.

Soaking in the smells and sights and sounds of that moment, Mellie let her eyes half close.

It *was* pure brightness, she thought.

Somewhere, quite near, was a soft, ringing sound— her bracelets touching as she raised a pastry to her lips. The silken swish of Aunt Estie's skirt caught the sunlight and held it in a shimmer of warmth. She tasted the sweetness of the pastry in her mouth, smooth on her tongue, and she felt the breathing nearness of Papa and Geem-Wah. Suddenly, in her heart was a singing, clear and strong—the strange, familiar song that at last was Mellie's own.